## DEADLY DEPTH CHARGE ATTACK!

The shattering crashes thumped through the water. They smashed at U-55 and rolled her half-over. Crockery smashed in the galley. The lights went out and Lindner immediately started going round screwing in fresh bulbs, phlegmatically.

The next pattern was just that much farther away to induce the crew of U-55 to imagine the Englishman was off on the wrong scent.

Wolz kept listening for that deadly pinging sound echoing against his steel hull. When it came he immediately altered course, speed and level. Three times he threw off the inhuman pinging, and three times the English picked him up again.

More depth charges sailed down . . .

*Also by Bruno Krauss in Sphere Books:*

SEA WOLF: STEEL SHARK
SEA WOLF: SHARK NORTH
SEA WOLF: SHARK PACK
SEA WOLF: SHARK HUNT

# Sea Wolf:
# Shark Africa

**BRUNO KRAUSS**

SPHERE BOOKS LIMITED
30/32 Gray's Inn Road, London WC1X 8JL

First published in Great Britain by Sphere Books Ltd. 1980
Copyright © Bruno Krauss 1980

Set in Monotype Times

Printed in Great Britain by
William Collins Sons & Co Ltd
Glasgow

# CHAPTER ONE

U-55 put her bows into the sea, lifted and shook like a sheep-dog and slung a bucketful of water into the face of Oberleutnant zur See Baldur Wolz. Wolz took the long thin cheroot from his mouth, looked at the soggy and disgusting mess and philosophically chucked it over the side. He wiped his face with a forefinger.

'And keep her on course, Obersteuermann,' he bellowed down into the tower. 'You're leting her head fall off.'

'Very good!'

Again U-55 put her bows under and reared like a charging horse. Water poured in a jumbled wash from her casing. Spume lifted high, white and ghostly against the quarter moon. Somewhere off to port lay the coast of Spain, to starboard and much closer lay Africa, and ahead waited Gibraltar and the Straits. After those – the Mediterranean . . .

The only trouble Wolz could see – and it was big trouble – to stop them entering the Med was the passage of the Straits.

Many attempted that hazardous journey and many failed.

The men were a trifle more jumpy than Wolz cared for. He had been ordered by BdU in the august and awe-inspiring person of Admiral Donitz to take U-55 into the Mediterranean. This Wolz would do, or – in the cant and phlegmatic phrase – die trying. Far too many U-boat men had died trying in this war which was now two years' old.

'Light – green twenty!'

Wolz whirled at the forward starboard-lookout's yell.

He stared over the starboard bow into darkness with the moon's glimmer silvering the wave tops. U-55 pitched down and up and everyone on the bridge moved easily with the rhythm. The breeze smelled warm and spicy, and the sea sloshed alongside, running spouting over the casing.

'Where away?' growled Wolz.

'Gone now, skipper. But it was there – I swear it.'

'You don't swear in my boat.'

'Very good!'

There was no need for answer; but discipline required it. All the men of U-55 were well aware of the skipper's ways and demands by now, ways and demands that made U-55 a happy boat.

Wolz checked the course again.

'Keep her steady,' he said again, letting the bite into his voice.

Spain remained neutral, over to port. Also ahead and to port stood Gibraltar. This was like putting your head into a trap. The British infested the Rock with their apes, and they had a nasty habit of putting destroyer patrols to sea to sink U-boats. They sent their aeroplanes out to drop depth charges on U-boats. Sailing in the vicinity of Gibraltar was not a healthy business for a U-boat.

There was no further sign of the enigmatic light.

Wolz felt that the lookout, Schmidt, had seen a light. He was a dependable quiet man from Hamburg, and if he said he had seen a light he had seen a light.

Ehrenberger, the First Watch Officer, shouted up through the tower.

'Permission to come on the bridge.'

Wolz looked around. 'Mueller – you go below.'

'Very good.'

The aft starboard lookout left his post, stretching, knuckling his red-rimmed eyes. He shook himself of water drops and then vanished down the hatch. Presently

Ehrenberger climbed up through the tower on to the bridge. Wolz was staring through his night glasses on Mueller's quarter.

'There might be a light up ahead to starboard, Kern,' Wolz greeted his Number One. 'If there is he's right close into shore.'

'Port's where the trouble-'ll come from, skipper.'

'Maybe.'

Everyone in the boat felt the tenseness and the jumpiness. They were a good crew, highly trained and successful. They had carried out a number of highly profitable patrols with Wolz in command. He had been very lucky to keep his cadre of officers intact, and the turnover in the ratings had been minimal. He had two Fahnrichs with him, and they were like mischievous puppies forever getting into scrapes. They would shape up. If they did not and they lived they'd probably end up on the Eastern Front. But all in all he was as well pleased with his command as he felt he would ever be. Now they were creeping along through enemy infested waters making the break through into the Med.

At any instant, death and destruction could burst upon them from the night.

'Talk about the Duke of Hell's riding boots,' grumbled Ehrenberger. 'Who'd be shining a light on a night like this?'

Wolz did not reply, contenting himself with a companionable grunt. Ehrenberger – who was called Kern although that was not his name – possessed the soul of a great fighter and the spirit of a dedicated U-boatman. Wolz could scarcely ask for more. He peered into the night, sweeping from aft through the beam to forrard and back aft again.

U-55 churned along, the twin diesels thrumming, the smell of blue exhaust smoke whiffed away on the salty breeze.

'The Chief's been talking to himself again, skipper.'

Ehrenberger was also looking out as he spoke; there was no room for idle eyes on the bridge of a U-boat in this man's war. 'His beard looked more red than a furnace. I think he is trying to quell incipient trouble somewhere among his pipes and valves.'

'If he can't, then no one can.'

As the L.I. – the Leitender Ingenieur – of the boat, Loeffler was the best Chief Engineering Officer Wolz could wish for. If there was a piece of string or a chunk of beeswax then Loeffler would keep the boat running somehow.

'Resume your watch, Kern,' said Wolz. 'I'll send Mueller up again. Think I'll find out what the Chief has on his mind.'

Dropping down through the hatch, Wolz promised himself that he would not be away from the bridge for more than ten minutes at the most. A U-boat could be sunk in less time than that.

The familiar warm fug of the boat met him as he dropped off the ladder into the control room. The maze of piping and levers and valves emphasised Ehrenberger's comments. The control room concentrated alertly on their tasks, and the boat ran sweetly. If she did not, with Loeffler as the Chief, then something somewhere was seriously wrong.

He went through the control room to the wardroom without even a glance at his own tiny curtained-off space that was laughingly referred to as the captain's cabin. Hellmuth Freyer, the Third Watch Officer, sat with his hands behind his neck, his head thrown back, his eyes fast closed, blissfully listening to his record. The Prelude to Act Three of Lohengrin sounded tinny and scratchy, and Freyer had the sound turned right down – on Wolz's orders.

Ludwig Riepold, the Second Officer, was fast asleep and Wolz let him lie. The two midshipmen were not about, and Wolz knew they were busy on tasks he had set them – one forrard in the fore ends trying to learn something about torpedoes, the other in the diesel engine room. He pushed through there now; but did not stop, going on into the electric motor room as the Chief's fiery beard was nowhere visible in the narrow space by the twin diesels. The noise racketted away, the light bit down, sweat and oil and pitch stank in the close air.

As he straightened up from ducking through the narrow round bulkhead door, Hans Guggenberger, the Elektro Obermaschinist, lying prone on the deck, jerked back with a yell. Bright fat blue sparks flew. The Chief, looming over the petty officer, made a caustic comment and then leaned down. In his grimy fist an enormous spanner gleamed.

'Not that one! Here – get this beauty around it – and careful. If that fracture increases – '

He looked up to see Wolz staring at him.

The big red beard bristled. Loeffler's square face showed anger and annoyance and a determination not to give into faulty workmanship.

'Trouble, Chief?'

'Yes, skipper. I'm checking out the extent. I'll be able to give you a full report – '

'What's the present position? We're on diesels now – '

'The shaft and oil drip here – well, I can run this motor for you – but it'll pack up in less than five minutes. The starboard one I wouldn't risk even looking at – '

'No electric propulsion?'

'Right.'

Wolz kept his sharp-featured, square face composed. The lines around his mouth and eyes were being graven in by life as a U-boatman. His immaculately combed blond hair shimmered golden in the lighting.

'So we can't dive?'

5

'No.'

'I see. Well, do what you can. How long?'

'That is what I'm trying to establish – '

'Let me know. And, Chief, make it fast. We may have to dive in a hurry – '

'I know. That's why I'm sweating.'

Going back through the stuffy cramped boat, Wolz reflected that they were both taking this emergency very casually. But, then, that was the only sane way to take it. No use in screaming and raving. Loeffler would do his utmost. That went without saying. The moment he could dive the boat, he would inform the commander. Wolz would have to wait.

Waiting. That was the be-all and end-all of U-boat warfare, it often seemed to him.

If an English destroyer picked them up now . . . Well, that was unlikely. The low silhouette of a U-boat on a night like this would be extraordinarily difficult to discern against the dark sea.

Back on the bridge he scanned the horizon, seeing the stars obscured by patchy invisible clouds.

'Any further report on that light?'

'No, skipper.'

'Very good. Carry on.'

U-55 moved through the sea, a long lean lethal steel shark. But she was, for the moment, denied entrance to her proper element.

Keeping a constant lookout imposed intolerable eye-strain and the men on the bridge changed over frequently during their watch. Rather have the men changing over lookout duty, with the consequent passage up and down through the tower, than have a man with red raw eyes desperately attempting a vigilance his body could no longer support. Four hours on watch, that was the regulations. Wolz changed his lookouts ten times or so in that period, and would cut that time period down

6

if conditions became very bad.

In dirty weather one problem was the short supply of wet-weather clothing. But even that had to be changed, particularly in bad weather. Life was not easy in the U-boat arm of the Kriegsmarine.

'Light! Green twenty!'

Wolz spun about.

He was just in time to see a narrow fan of pure white light shine out across the jumbled sea. It vanished even as he saw it.

'A lighthouse?' He shook his head. 'Don't they know there's a war on?'

'Not them,' said Ehrenberger. 'It's all over for them.'

'Yes.'

An accurate bearing was taken on the source of the light and as U-55 sailed on so the changing bearings were plotted. The boat was trimmed down, with partially-flooded tanks, which made life on the bridge in this jumbled sea less than comfortable. Wolz scrutinised the darkness over to the starboard bow, and then swung about to check all around the compass. The clouds patched the stars with black gaps. The breeze whisked drops of water across him and he made no attempt to jam a fresh cigar into his mouth.

The lookouts changed according to a strict rota, so that there was no commotion of men passing through the tower in a clumsy rush. Mueller's trick was up and he went below and his relief came on to the bridge, giving a quick and involuntary shiver as the night air struck him.

Over on the port bow the darkness lay like an opaque and stifling blanket. The cream of the sea past the saddle tanks washed away aft. Vision was lost too closely for comfort.

Wolz stared.

His eyes were keen. He was used by now to spotting

sightings before the lookouts, and he had been forced to understand that it was no good punishing men for not having as keen eyesight as their commander.

Was that a dark shape out there, a blur of shadows? Was that a real outline or a mere trick of tired eyes?

Very carefully he shut his eyes. He counted six. Then, opening his eyes again he turned his head a little sideways and, pretending to himself that he was not really looking, he took in the picture presented to the corners of his eyes.

Yes! A shape, a definite shape, a hard outline in the shrouding darkness . . .

'Red ninety,' he said in a quiet voice. 'What do you see?'

The two port lookouts stared. Their hands wrapped around the big night glasses.

Finally: 'A ship, skipper . . .' And: 'Something out there . . .'

Wolz satisfied himself that the erratic shape he had first seen had hardened into substance. It had to be a ship. And, because the ship was running without lights, it had to be English.

An English destroyer, ghosting along, parallel to their course . . .

'He can't have seen us, skipper,' said Ehrenberger.

'No. I think you're right. Otherwise he'd be roaring in and throwing everything he has at us.'

The quarter moon was completely hidden by cloud. There was no real chance the English lookouts would spot them. But the bow-wave from U-55's sleek steel prow and the creamy wash of water along her saddle tanks might just be visible, might just betray them.

With a full understanding of what the move entailed, Wolz reduced speed. U-55 ran more easily and that spume of white along her steel flanks flattened and died.

Temptation beckoned Baldur Wolz.

His orders were to break through into the Mediterranean. Hitler's Italian allies, in the odd parlance of the times, were still in trouble. DAK – the Deutsches Afrika Korps – under the command of General Rommel had been sent to the assistance of the Duce's hard-pressed troops. And the English were merrily sinking the supply ships vital to the continuance of the war in Africa.

One of Wolz's tasks in the Central Sea would be to sink the English ships carrying supplies to the British forces and thus even up the score. But – but the temptation, now, was to order an alteration of course and line up that infuriating shadow that kept at the limit of visibility and slip a couple of eels up his jacket. That would set him up nicely.

Also, it would send the balloon up. Every patrolling destroyer for miles would know, at once, that U-boats were operating in the Straits.

And he had been ordered to break into the Med without any fuss. Just get in and interrupt the flow of supplies to Malta and Tobruk and anywhere else HQ in Salamis thought best.

Wolz gripped the coaming of the bridge and stared. The wind-deflector occasionally caught the odd slap of spume; but the bridge was appreciably drier now. To sink that shadow – sinking shadows was not his business. Sinking English transports and freighters was.

Temptation – he had always thought himself reasonably clear headed at resisting temptation. But, sometimes . . .

Like Lottie, and Heidi, and Mariza – and all the others . . .

At least, Marlene's temptation had not bitten . . .

Speaking very quietly, he said : 'Port twenty. Steer oh-six-oh.'

'Port twenty. Steer oh-six-oh.'

Ehrenberger swung about to look at him in the darkness.

In complete explanation, Wolz said: 'We can replenish our eels in Salamis.'

At least, that might be a complete explanation to Baldur Wolz. To any reasonably cautious skipper the idea of wantonly attacking a destroyer was hideous nonsense, absolute suicide. Don't start digging about with your fingers in a cave inhabited by a conger-eel . . . But Wolz felt a calm competence flowing from U-55, a competence he now believed he shared. If his boat could not sink any other ship with a spread at this distance, then no other boat in the entire service could.

He did not thus boast. He felt this to be a fact warranted by results.

Ehrenberger nodded to himself and went down to the tower to sit on the saddle-seat of the attack periscope.

Wolz spoke a few quiet words to the lookouts. It might be unnecessary; but he wanted their eyes fixed on their quarters and not all gawping at the target.

He looked again himself. The shadow seemed to him, definite though it was, to remain small. U-55 was edging across the gap, her sharp bows swinging gently across to narrow the angle for the torpedoes. The range was coming down. Wolz frowned. The range as indicated and the size of that hard-edged shadow did not correspond in his mind.

The smell of the sea washed over him, the sound of the waves and the feel of the breeze on his cheek. He checked again.

He bent to the pipe.

'What do you make of him, Kern?'

The First Officer's voice sounded cautious.

'Difficult to pick him up, skipper. If he is a destroyer he is not very large.'

'No.'

Wolz did not care much for the idea that he would be loosing off an expensive torpedo at a fishing boat.

Yet to make any closer attempt at identification would

be taking a risk he would not accept. He had to make up his mind. And he had to make it up fast.

Well, like any military man, he could take refuge in his orders.

'Skipper.'

'Yes, Kern.'

'He's definitely not a destroyer. Can't be. Much too small.'

'Yes. I agree. Cancel attack. Starboard twenty. Steer oh-eight-oh.'

'Starboard twenty. Steer oh-eight-oh.'

The quartermaster on the wheel brought U-55's head around. Wolz stared at that infuriating shadow over there. Criminal stupidity to waste torpedoes on a fishing boat . . .

The sea before his eyes, the harsh metal of his boat, the figures of the lookouts, all were abruptly bathed in a violent blaze of white light.

He could see the shadow of the U-boat spread before him on the sea, limned clearly. He could even see the black silhouette of himself, his head clear over the bridge.

'That light!'

U-55 lay bathed in light, naked, shown up, pitilessly exposed.

In the next instant a dot of red light winked from the shadow over there. Wolz heard the crack of the shot and saw the shell burst in the sea a hands-breadth from his fragile saddle tanks.

'We're a clay pipe in a shooting gallery!'

'And we cannot dive!'

Another shot smashed out and the explosion burst on the wintergarden. Invisible chunks of metal whined past Wolz's head.

'Full ahead both!' he roared and the sea off the port beam lifted and broke with a stunning concussion to slash all across the bridge of U-55.

# CHAPTER TWO

Lieutenant Arnold Blackie, RN, commanding HMS *Lady Lucy*, bellowed in his fiercest voice down from his tiny bridge.

'Shoot straight! Hit the bastard! We've caught him with his pants down!'

The trawler's four-inch gun cracked out again. Smoke belched, acrid in the darkness. Over there and illuminated as though in a shooting gallery the ugly silhouette of a damned U-boat ghosted through the water. The splashes of *Lady Lucy*'s four-incher showed like spectres, white towers shot through with glints and streaks of shadow. One shot had hit home.

Lieutenant Blackie was sure of that. It had hit aft of the conning tower and he could swear a gun had been dismounted.

At the gun the gunlayer, Seaman Bill Wesker, brought his sights on with the finicky precision he had been accustomed to use six months ago on laying a course of bricks just right in the alignment of the wall. A good brickie, Bill Wesker, and now he was a sailor in one of His Majesty's requisitioned trawlers and laying a four-inch gun with a Jerry U-boat in his sights.

The gun belched and smoke blew back. The jar smashed up Wesker's feet and he was impatiently waiting for the crew to fling the breech open and eject the spent cartridge case and slam in a fresh round. The clangs gonged out in order and the orders snapped out fiercely. This was no drill – not now.

Again Wesker fired and this time – he would swear! –

he hit the Jerry smack in the guts.

*Lady Lucy* surged to the swell and Wesker swung his gun with the movement, holding the sights on.

Up on the bridge Arnold Blackie slammed a fist down, wildly excited. He wanted to take off his cap and wave it in the air, urging his men on. Come on! Come on!

And, still the U-boat had not returned the fire.

Sub-Lieutenant George Watson crouched at the stripped Lewis on the bridge. He had been out of grammar school for a few years; they seemed a lifetime and schooldays ten lifetimes ago. King Alfred had seen to that. Now he lined up the sights and pressed the trigger, willing the shots to sweep that ugly conning-tower bridge clean.

'Keep shooting!'

But the light snapped off as abruptly as it had switched on.

Everyone blinked in the sudden darkness.

'Where is he?' And: 'Keep on the bearing – shoot!'

The four-inch hammered out again and the stripped Lewis stuttered wildly. No answering fire came in, no tell-tale red wink of flame to tell *Lady Lucy*'s gunners the point of aim.

Blackie ripped out a quick steering order and *Lady Lucy* swung towards the vanished U-boat, heading down on a south-easterly run. But Blackie had no real hope.

*Lady Lucy* was a whisker over one hundred and twenty feet long, her gross tonnage four hundred and fifty or so; she'd been built in 1935 and the Navy had requisitioned her in 1939. She could, if the engine room staff put their fingers in their ears and prayed, stoke up to eleven knots.

That damned U-boat out there was racing away on the surface at sixteen or so knots.

Blackie stared through the darkness, his eyes still flecked and flaked by the after images of the light. The light had given them the U-boat; they just hadn't had the wherewithal to sink it.

He would feel forward south-east until he felt he had reached the track of the U-boat. Asdic simply pinged out, empty and hollow. No welcomed answering echo came bouncing back to indicate they had a contact.

The U-boat was on the surface. That was why.

Sub-Lieutenant George Watson pushed his cap back on his head. He walked across to join his captain – a very short walk indeed.

'I got him all right, I think – but he was lit up like a target in a shooting gallery and then he was gone into the shadows.'

'The four-inch hit him, George. I'm confident of that. We've given him something to think about, if nothing else.'

'Given him a headache, sir.'

Blackie felt a sudden withdrawal of the tenseness. The U-boat was gone and they wouldn't see the murdering bastard again.

'No, Number One. Not a headache. I hope an ache much further down . . .'


Baldur Wolz wiped the thick blood from his face.

The aft port lookout, young Wissel who came from Emden and who although a thin and gangling fellow always had a cheery grin, screamed and thrashed about against the harsh iron of the bridge. It was his blood that Wolz wiped away.

Wissel's left arm was somewhere in the briny. From the gashed and ghastly stump the thick blood pulsed, the ragged edging of white and blue and leather soaked dark.

'Get him below!' shouted Wolz.

The shell splinter that had removed Wissel's arm had been from the last shot fired, exploding in the sea and flinging its deadly freight upwards. They'd been lucky the shot had not penetrated their saddle tank. And poor

Wissel had been in the way.

Well, it could have been anyone.

It could have been Oblt z. S. Baldur Wolz.

As the screaming youngster was rapidly manhandled below where the new Sanitatsobermaat would attend to him, Wolz reflected that it might have a most salutary effect on war-mongers if they could see some of the results of their handiwork.

Suppose the fat citizens of Germany could see Wissel now, see him screaming, see his ashen face wet with sweat, see the awful hole in his shoulder? Suppose the cinemas showed pictures like that instead of the synthetic confections of the Wehrmacht photographers, with waving flags and rumbling panzers and marching jack-boots? Suppose the English could see pictures of their own men hideously maimed?

There had been an exhibition in London, just before the war, of these so-called atrocity pictures. Photographs from the First World War, and the Spanish Civil War, pictures of men blown up and shot and de-gutted. Pictures, too, of women and children cut down by the high-flying bombers. Dick Mitchell had mentioned the exhibition, and its avowed aims of stopping war and of the way people refused to see that and saw only the affront to their susceptibilities of showing indecent pictures of maimed soldiers.

Wolz would not think about Dick Mitchell. He had been a friend, and an Englishman, a sailor, and he had been killed. If the people at home could see what death was really like in war, with none of this romantic non-sense about gently sinking to earth with not a speck of blood and a resigned smile on the face, as though the dying man was thinking only and gladly of duty to his fatherland, why, then, perhaps, the politicians would not so easily find brave young men willing to rush off to be killed.

These sour thoughts filled his head as U-55 surged on into the darkness.

That ship back there had been a tiny patrol craft of some kind, a trawler, probably. Hardly worth a torpedo – and yet she had wreaked this havoc.

Wolz could not allow these thoughts to deflect him from what he clearly saw as his duty. England had lost the war and had not realised or admitted that yet. If he could make the English see the truth, see sense, then he would. And the only way he could do that was by sinking ships, piling up the tonnages sunk so that England must cry quarter.

And now the Führer had marched the nation against Russia.

Well, there was no doubt in Wolz's mind that any good German could see the necessity for that confrontation. But he doubted that this was exactly the best time for it to have happened.

With a curt word to Ehrenberger he ducked down through the hatch and went to see how Wissel fared.

The Sanitatsobermaat had sedated the wounded man and was doing what he could about the extensive hole. The arm had been blown clean off. The packing and bandaging looked oddly white and sterile in the gleaming oily interior of the boat. Into the smells of machine oil and diesel fuel and pitch and cabbages and human sweat the raw stench of blood added the final note, underlying the agony they must all endure.

'Will he be all right?'

'If the shock does not kill him, skipper.'

After Reche's breakdown, U-55 had acquired Sanitatsobermaat Heinz Otterndorf. A big, easy-going man with a red bull neck, he came from Bavaria and intended, when the war was over, to carry on his training as a vet. Privately, Wolz considered Otterndorf to be lucky he wasn't caring for horses in Russia.

'Do what you can for him, Otterndorf.'

'Very good. He'll be discharged the service, that's certain.'

'I think he'd sooner have his arm back and be in.'

Otterndorf nodded, lapping bandages, his tongue wedged between his teeth at the final finicky moments. The smell of medical chemicals stank in the close air.

With a feeling of relief, Wolz climbed back to the bridge.

U-55 was a happy ship, and he intended to keep her that way. The quicker he could unload poor Wissel the better.

His humanity told him that. His concern as a U-boat commander told him that he needed to get into port to carry out a thorough inspection.

The Chief reported no damage that was vital.

The aft 2-cm had been blown to kingdom come. The wintergarden was a wreck of twisted steel. But all that could be fixed. The boat still lacked electric propulsion and dawn was coming and with the dawn would come the air patrols from Gibraltar.

It was going to be a tricky six hours.

The breeze was veering and the sea was going down. The roll and surge of U-55 smoothed out. The darkness remained intense when the clouds shut down, relieved in ghostly streamers of pale light as the moon intermittently broke through the grey blanket.

Dawn was not far off now.

'How's it coming, Chief?'

'It isn't, skipper. We have a real devil here. We're getting iron-filings out of the feeds –'

Wolz felt his jaws stiffen.

He felt the red rage burst all through him, and he trembled.

'Sabotage?'

'I'd say so. Although how it was done beats me.'

'I'll have a few words to say to the flotilla commander in Lorient, believe you me.'

'Add a few choice comments from me, too, skipper.'

'As soon as you can, Chief. Dawn's not far off.'

'Very good!'

As Wolz stood on his bridge his thoughts beat like black vulture wings. Germany was committed now to fight Russia with England still undefeated although beaten to her knees – and the ominous evidence of sabotage to his U-boat indicated all too clearly that the occupied territories were still disaffected – to put it no stronger.

All he could do was carry out his orders. He had to assist General Rommel in his African struggle.

To do that meant, for a U-boat commander, sinking enemy ships carrying supplies and comfort.

This, Baldur Wolz promised himself, he would do.

A faint roseate streaking appeared low in the sky ahead. Wolz squinted his tired eyes at the radiance. When that died the darkness would be more intense than ever. After that, the dawn would herald the first vultures from the Rock seeking their prey.

The delay that had prevented them from beginning their run through at the time Wolz originally desired looked now as though it was going to be costly. Perhaps prohibitively costly. Again Wolz looked ahead at that rosy-fingering against the gloom.

If he dived at dawn he'd have no propulsive power. The dynamics of a boat in her usual trim demanded forward movement to provide the pressure on the planes to keep her down. There were other ways. Wolz would use whatever was necessary in his armoury of expertise; he knew that it would be suicidal to remain on the surface in daylight in reach of the Rock's aircraft.

At least – that was the theory . . .

He bent to the mouthpiece again.

'Chief?'

After a moment Loeffler's voice came through.

'Skipper?'

He sounded tired. Well, they were all tired.

'How's it coming?'

'We've stripped the muck out. Give me another hour.'

Wolz digested that. He lifted his head and stared broodingly at the eastern horizon.

'I may have to dive before then. Be ready to flood up promptly.'

'But –'

'I know, Chief. But the two-centimetre's been blown to smithereens.'

'I see.'

'Yes. We'll just go down.'

'Very good!'

Wolz turned away and let his gaze rest on the lookouts, each in turn, checking by the way the man's head was held, the grip on his glasses, the stance of his body, just how alert they were. U-112 had lost a lookout. The poor devil had gone to sleep with his glasses at his eyes and when the boat submerged he'd simply washed off. In the scurry to get below, no one had noticed him. Wolz had not been in command.

He let his mind drift for a betraying instant to the ever-recurring wonder of Trudi von Hartstein. The way she had slowly undone each little button, each little shiny black button, one after another, and the way the grey dress had fallen aside. He would remember that with pity and with tenderness and with a raging anger that such things were thought necessary between them – then. Well, he'd driven her to the Bodensee. He'd been turned off, summarily, by her friends, hard, tough people, unknown to Wolz.

What Trudi was up to had come a little clearer, and had made Wolz even more afraid for her safety.

The eastern horizon shimmered with a soft greyness, a gentle erasure of the blackness and the star glitter.

Soon the radiance lightened and warmed with pink and orange streaks. A bar of chocolate-coloured cloud lay across the sea. Now he could discern the hard iron of the boat, the condensation on the steel, the outlines firming and taking on their own familiar day shapes.

He turned to look aft.

Up there, from the paling sky, would come those who sought to kill everyone in the U-boat.

The line of the coast to southward offered no help.

The sea stretched about them, calming now and moving with a sensation new to men fresh from the Atlantic. The colour of that sea was different, also. It was warmer, bluer, more sparkling. But, for all that romantic idea, it was still the final enemy.

When the sighting at last came, Wolz realised they had been running for much longer than he might have expected.

They were naked on the sea. A narrow steel shark, plunging along with their white wash spreading and forming into a wide creamy wake, they were visible for miles.

'Clear the bridge!'

He squinted up. Twin-engined, stubby, powerful – probably a Hudson. The men were falling down through the hatch, one and one-fifth seconds per man.

'Flood! Dive!'

He went down last. The hatch slammed shut with a spray of water splashing down on to his upturned face.

Powerless, U-55 sank like a stone into the warm waters of the Mediterranean. Above them, the enemy aeroplane came sniffing down like a ferret at a rabbit hole.

# CHAPTER THREE

Baldur Wolz was never a man to praise himself. If he thought he had made a mistake he could be very unforgiving, very hard on himself.

Now he felt he had calculated a tricky problem with a degree of nicety. He had held on his course for as long as he could, powering along on diesels. He had dived with plenty of time to spare. The aeroplane might have spotted them with the whiteness of their wake to betray them; but his last sight of the Hudson seemed to him to confirm she was remaining steady on course.

She might have caught a last glimpse as he dived and come sniffing around – rather like that ferret at the rabbit hole – but even with the damned transparency of Mediterranean water, U-55 ought to be deep enough to escape detection.

Ought to be – one could never *see* in a U-boat . . .

Wolz hungered for a view of the sea's surface from the vantage point of pilot and observers in that Hudson up there.

The trouble with the Mediterranean was that the water was just too perfect.

Out in the cold North Sea a U-boat could remain undetected from the air when she ran along at periscope depth. The keen eyes in the searching aircraft could see deeper into the water in the Atlantic and a boat must submerge enough to compensate. But the Med!

He knew he must keep his boat down deep if he was to escape observation.

Looking down into the water the men flying in their

dogged patrol patterns would see the betraying shape of a U-boat, the leanly-swollen shark shape, as it glided deep below the surface.

But, in the boat, no one could look up into the air and see the stalking nemesis, for they were far below periscope depth.

U-55 had a strange feel about her.

'Those electric motors,' said Freyer, shaking his head. He had turned his gramophone record off. He knew, now, when enough was enough.

Wolz stood in the control room and he could not stop himself from slightly cocking his head up, as though he could see and hear better what was going on in the air above him.

The helmsman reported no bite on the rudder.

Presently the gyro compass indicated that east lay off their starboard beam. A few minutes later east had shifted to their starboard quarter.

When east was indicated as dead astern, Wolz wondered if U-55 would go on spinning around and around. But they steadied up on that bearing. U-55 was being carried along in the current stern first.

Water continually poured from the Atlantic into the Mediterranean, one of the factors that made it difficult for a boat to get out. The force and power of the current varied; but Wolz knew they were being swept along stern first, spat from the Strait like a cork from a bottle.

What a way to run a U-boat!

Drifting stern-first into the area where he was supposed to live up to his reputation as a Sea Wolf!

Stern-first – it made the blood run cold.

'Gives you a queasy sensation in the guts, skipper,' said Ehrenberger.

Wolz nodded, not smiling.

'Seasick, Kern?'

'Not seasick, skipper. It reminds me of the time – off

the Elbe estuary – when we lost our oars. We drifted all night. Nasty.'

'Very nasty.'

'Still, there were compensations.'

Wolz lifted his eyebrows. They were making conversation as U-55 drifted helplessly stern first caught in the grip of the current.

'You mean the commander didn't find out?'

'Oh, no. I mean that Karin – who lost the oars, the dear girl – felt most contrite. She did her best to make it up to me.'

'Lucky man.'

'Oh, yes, Skipper, lucky. Still, the thwarts of an open boat aren't the best of places for – '

'The back of a motor car?'

Kern laughed.

'I'm old-fashioned. A nice thick mattress suits me.'

And U-55 drifted on, bows last, drifted on into the Mediterranean and whatever of adventure awaited her there.

Because of the clarity of the water the Med was unforgiving to submarines. The British had lost a large number of boats already, and no one liked being a submariner in these waters.

'It's so undignified,' burst out Freyer, intense, annoyed, as though ready to blame everything on the Valkyrean fates whose musical tones issued from his sacred records. 'I feel stupid about it.'

'You said it, Helmuth.' Ehrenberger was mindful of his duty as the IWO to keep the youngsters firmly in their places. 'Stupid is as stupid does.'

Freyer had the sense to compose his features to stony disciplined impassiveness and to snap the expected response.

'Very good!'

'Anyway, Helmuth,' said Ehrenberger in a more soothing tone of voice, as though he wished to remind Freyer that the duty part done with, he shared the Third Officer's point of view, 'we don't have enough battery life to sail through the Strait submerged all the way, as you very well know. So we have to do it in quick stabs.'

'And,' pointed out Wolz, 'the current is giving us a free ride.'

'A free ride to where is what I'd like to know.'

A silence fell. No one wished to comment on that conundrum.

Wolz glanced at his watch. The hour was up.

Now came one of those tedious little niceties of command. A problem of protocol, ethics and discipline. Should he go and stir Loeffler up, or should he wait, well-knowing the Chief would report the moment the repairs were finished?

Indeed, it was a trifle; but of such trifles are the cares of command constructed.

That fiercer-red beard would be jammed down into the insides of some complicated piece of apparatus, and Loeffler would be concentrating absolutely devotedly on what he was doing. He must have completely missed the passage of time, and had not realised the hour he had promised was up.

So, all right, then. Wolz had trust in his LI – he had to have trust. He would not worry the Chief –

The whistle spat and Loeffler's voice said:

'Skipper?'

'Chief?'

'Another fifteen minutes.'

'Very good.'

But the way Wolz spoke those over-familiar words indicated his confidence and his commander's gratitude. If the Chief hadn't called – but, then, the Chief had.

A quarter of an hour later the ready to run signal came through and then the thrilling almost unheard vibration of the motors. That sound was just about beneath the audible threshold; but it was there, making itself aware to a U-boat man by a trembling fibrillation inside, it seemed, his teeth. Odd. But comforting.

Baldur Wolz drew a breath.

They were under control once more, and when he gave a steering order U-55 would respond to her helm and turn on to the required course. Like a racehorse responsive to the commands of his jockey, the boat lived and breathed and once again had a purpose in life. Even if, as it was, that purpose was the purpose of death . . .

'Periscope depth.'

'Periscope depth.'

U-55 nosed towards the east and rose smoothly through the water.

If that Hudson – if it had been a Hudson – had remained on patrol, suspiciously circling a possible sighting, then U-55 would be lifting into trouble. Wolz wanted to know.

The depth gauges recorded their ascent. The hiss of compressed air sounded muffled. He held to the cord of the sky search periscope. The control room personnel concentrated on their instruments, quietly. The Cox'n would bear down harshly on any idiot who fouled up now. Hans Lindner, the Oberbootsman, like the LI, was a comfort to Wolz.

The depths were called off and the periscope broke clear of the surface.

Wolz took a rapid three-sixty-degree sweep of sea and sky.

He could see no sign of an aircraft.

The day looked promising, bright and cheerful, with the clouds shredding away, high and remote. It would be a nice day to go swimming up there.

'Down periscope. A hundred metres.'

U-55 slid back to the depths and continued eastwards,

leaving the Strait, heading out into the Mediterranean.

The two Fahnrichs had to be kept occupied, and Wolz made sure in an unobtrusive way that Ehrenberger bore down on them hard enough but not over-harshly. The two midshipmen were going to have to shoulder burdens of responsibility in the boat sooner or later, and Wolz wanted to make sure of them first.

One, Friedrich Thumen, looked to be a shambling bear of a fellow, with an easy smile and brown hair that would not lie flat. He appeared to be slow; but Wolz had seen him dodge when the torpedo-handling crew thought a chain was slipping and had yelled warnings. Then, Fahnrich Thumen had leaped aside as nimbly as a mountain goat. He'd handle the eels and learn to know every single fiddly detail of the torpedoes. And, after that, he could be sent about further duties.

The other Fahnrich, Dietrich Jagow, was an altogether different proposition. His blond hair was as golden and smoothly brushed as Wolz's own. His face was pear-shaped, heavy and yet taut of skin over bone, and perhaps the most odd thing of all, his nose was large and fleshy with a pendulous bulb at the tip. His skin was sallow and shone. He held himself erect, tightly-strung, like a fiddle-string.

On his finger he wore a golden ring with oak leaves and an enamel swastika.

Someone had remarked on it, and had added that U-boatmen did not favour rings.

'The Führer – ' began Jagow.

The spirits in the boat seemed to sigh and shrink.

'You catch your hand by that ring,' Jagow was told, 'don't come whining to us to find your damned finger for you.'

Wolz could do without dedicated Nazis in his boat. He'd suffered from their ill-timed and scornful enthusiasms before.

The watches changed and, assured that the boat ran smoothly, Wolz took himself off to his green-curtained cabin. The expected report to BdU would be sent. Right now he needed to catch up on all the lost sleep of the past few days.

But, naturally, he could not sleep.

He lay on his bunk and stared at the overhead. He had heard that the warm weather in the Med could be much more cheerful in a boat, preventing the worst excesses of cold and condensations; but he had also been told it could be a curse with the temperature shooting up beyond humanly-tolerable limits.

This, the people of U-55 would find out.

He just hoped Ehrenberger would not rub Jagow up the wrong way in any stupid fashion. With a third officer aboard the two midshipmen were along to be shown the ropes. And a Nazi would want to do everything in the way he had been indoctrinated. The Kriegsmarine had not been blessed with many Nazis so far, and for this the navy was truly grateful.

That swastika ring . . .

Cousin Siegfried would usually take off his own Death's-Head ring when he visited home. Wolz wasn't sure just why Siegfried should do this, although the ring was always in place if Siegfried wore the correct uniform. The SS were particular about these matters, as particular as Wolz was about the running of his U-boat.

The strange thing was – the heartening thing was – that Wolz had remained on friendly terms with his three cousins – his three male cousins. The female cousin, that gorgeous and ravishing Cousin Lisl for whom he had secretly hungered over the years, had opened up astonishing vistas for him.

He could feel grateful that he had been very lucky to have been taken in by a family with whom he got on. His father had been run down and his U-boat sunk by a criminally stupid German minesweeper right at the tail end of the last war. His mother had died soon after, and Baldur Wolz had been brought up with his aunt and uncle at the schloss. Now Manfred was flying his Messerschmitts in Russia, Siegfried was driving on and on never-endingly into the steppes in his panzers, and Helmut was – well, Helmut was doing whatever it was the Gestapo thought necessary to win the war.

He was never going to get to sleep like this. His tiredness would not let him relax. The feel of the boat about him, purring with power like a satisfied lioness, comforted him. He rolled off the bunk and, knuckling his eyes, pulled the green curtain open and rolled off to see poor Wissel.

The man was out of danger, the Sanitatsobermaat said, as well as he could judge.

'I stopped off the blood channels and did everything that could be done in these circumstances.' Sanitatsobermaat Otterndorf shook his head under his commander's scrutiny. 'At least, we have reasonable medical supplies – I'd have had to chuck sea water over the stump otherwise – '

'Some stump.'

Otterndorf looked down on Wissel, whose face had fallen in, like a collapsing tent. He breathed slowly and shallowly.

'Yes.'

'They're never going to fix him with a wooden arm, are they?'

'Highly probable, skipper. German medical science is the best in the world. They'll give him a wooden arm he can use with confidence.'

'Yes.'

'After all, we have a great deal of experience.' Otterndorf spoke with brisk confidence. He seemed entirely unaware of what he was really saying.

'Yes,' said Wolz, rather heavily. 'And we're likely to have a lot more.'

After a few more words, Wolz left. Movement had to be restricted in the boat to keep a trim. He went back to his cabin and lay down on the bunk. When he closed his eyes he saw, limned in a pure white fire, the naked body of a woman, her arms held out to him beckoningly, her ravaged face tear-streaked, gaunt with sadness. He rolled his head to the side; but she remained facing him, stretching out her arms appealingly. Her lips were very red.

He opened his eyes.

Then he climbed off the bunk and crawled through into the control-room and sat down under the blue lamp over the chart table. The hydrophone room's reports came in with a uniform negative. The air seemed to stifle into his head; yet they had not been running submerged for all that long.

The Cox'n, Hans Lindner, came through with a big coffee pot and Wolz took the proffered cup. Lindner filled the cup with a practised trajectory. The coffee steamed. It would be good coffee, French coffee, specially procured for the U-boat arm of the Kriegsmarine.

'At least, they do what they can,' said Lindner.

'Yes.'

'A pity about Wissel. It'll mean changing the watch bill again.'

'We'll manage somehow, Cox'n – anyway, we may pick up a replacement in Salamis.'

'The quicker the better, then, skipper.'

'Yes.'

Navy Group South at Salamis operated the German U-boats in the Med. The English traffic to Malta had to be stopped so that Malta could be taken out of the battle. From Malta, so Wolz had been informed in intelligence briefings, the English submarines carried on a crippling war against the German and Italian convoys to Africa.

If the British were to be thrown out of North Africa, as seemed to be the general belief, then Rommel must have all the support the Kriegsmarine could give him.

Rommel's name had come up in conversation with Cousin Siegfried when they'd been out for a day's hard walking.

'Very clever with panzers,' Siegfried said, striding along. 'Come on, Baldur, keep up! You navy types have no legs for marching.'

'I'm not a Pomeranian Grenadier, Siegfried.'

The trees were brilliant with leaf, green and glowing in the sunshine. The air smelled like the most expensive Paris perfumes. Birds chirruped away, filling every crevice with sound. Wolz would remember the birds singing when he was a hundred metres down.

'Rommel has done wonders in Libya, Baldur. But he has his enemies – oh, I'm not betraying any secrets.'

'He's an army man.'

Siegfried slashed his walking stick in the air, glancing at Wolz.

'Not SS or Navy? No. Quite.'

Very carefully, as they crossed a rutted road and struck along the shoulder of the hill beneath the trees, Wolz said : 'If the Italians – '

'Them!'

'If they'd been able to handle the English by themselves – '

'They couldn't even handle the Greeks.'

'That's what I was going to say. Rommel could have done with the troops we sent to the Balkans, surely?'

Siegfried again cocked an eye at his cousin. He cleared his throat, and strode on. Wolz wondered what had been said to occasion this.

Suddenly, Siegfried halted. He half-turned and waited for Wolz to catch him. He jammed his stick into the soft dry earth.

'There's a song the English sing. Strictly against rules and regulations, Baldur, I know; but it has been heard. It is good for a laugh. A small laugh.'

'Yes?'

'One line – "Frilly white skirts play the deuce with black shirts" – you get the play on "deuce" and "duce"?'

'My English will do for that, Siegfried.'

'No offence, no offence. Well?'

'Amusing. And the English sing this? Remarkable.'

'I wish I could find the heart to laugh. This Balkan business is bad for us. Tying up men we need.'

'Agreed. Rommel – '

Siegfried neatly decapitated a flower with his stick. He used it like a sabre.

'Oh, yes, Baldur. For Rommel.'

The crest of the hill revealed the white road and the trees bowering the schloss ahead. The whole view could give a man an ache in his heart when he recalled it in later times.

Siegfried swung his stick. 'And the delectable Mariza?'

'Ah, now, cousin, you have hit upon a mystery.'

'A mystery? You mean you haven't . . . What is it you U-boatmen say, something to do with a U-boat's periscope and asparagus?'

Wolz laughed.

'We call the periscope the spargel. It's slang, silly; but you know how important slang is in the services.'

'Assuredly. And this Mariza . . . ?'

'Your father's personal and private secretary. Charming.'

'No more?'

'What more should there be?'

Wolz wasn't going to let on to Siegfried the romps that Mariza and her racy friends got up to. That silly game they played where they asked questions and if the correct answer was not forthcoming then you paid a forfeit. The forfeit Mariza and her friends preferred was the removal of an item of clothing. They were most annoyed if you answered the question correctly.

And, looking at Mariza Kalman you'd never guess in a thousand years that she could ever play such a game.

Talking companionably they walked down the hill, still at Siegfried's Grenadier pace. He swung the stick now like a marshal's baton. The roofs of the schloss, glinting with a patina that had grown over the rich and lush years in this wealthy land, slowly sank out of sight behind the trees. They crossed the little wooden bridge ver the stream and paused with their elbows spread out on the polished wood to look down. They did not see any fish.

'Have you seen Trudi von Hartstein on any of your leaves, Baldur?'

The question came straight out, like a punch from the shoulder.

'Not recently.'

'No more have I. The place seems deserted. Odd. I wonder where she can have got to – her and her mother the baroness?'

'Everybody seems to be shifting about now, Siegfried. It's the damned war.'

'I hope Manfred has some good news to cheer us up –'

'He's coming on leave?'

'Oh, yes, he's coming on leave. Creating havoc as usual.'

'Good. I hadn't heard.'

'You know Manfred, everything high speed, always on the go.'

'Well, if he brings his Luftwaffe friends, and your SS comrades are at the schloss, also –'

'Why do you never bring your navy friends home, Baldur?'

That casual use of the word home did not strike at

Wolz's susceptibilities. He regarded his uncle's schloss as his home, for he had known no other – apart from the stinking steel tube of a U-boat's pressure hull.

'Willi couldn't come, and Rudi is off in a canoe somewhere doing mad and heroic things against the English.'

'Always the war, and always the English. I could wish the SS had had time to smarten them up.'

'I could wish we were not fighting them – '

Siegfried stopped striding on and, once again, turned to look closely at his cousin.

'I didn't mean it in the way you might think, Siegfried. A friend – someone I knew in the Royal Navy – he was killed – '

'Better him than you. That's our job, now.'

'I know. But – ' Wolz found he could not go on to tell Siegfried of the details of the death of Dick Mitchell. That oaf Forstner who had, fortunately for himself, been killed in killing Mitchell, was of that order of semi-humanity whose continued existence should be seriously questioned.

'And, anyway, Baldur,' Siegfried said, with a sudden lift in his voice, obviously just remembering. 'I heard that Rudi had been given a larger U-boat, ocean-going – seems he did rather well in his little boat. What d'you call them – canoes?'

'Type Two's – dugout canoes. Yes. I'm glad. At least I'm glad for Rudi. But he's such a madman – well, you know.'

Rudi von Falkensbach, as harum-scarum as a cadet as he had been as a Fahnrich and, from the letters Wolz received and read between the lines, still was as an Oberleutnant z. S., had proved a staunch comrade. Wolz's regret was that they could not see more of each other; but the demands of the service had prevented that. Now they commanded their own boats and had not been posted to the same flotilla, they could see each other only when their leaves coincided.

'I've missed Rudi's last letters, then. I wonder which flotilla they'll send him to – he's bound to be posted to one of the Biscay bases. If it's Lorient – why, we'll lay the place in ruins, between us!'

Siegfried laughed as they climbed over the fence using the old short cut they'd always used, many a time grazing a knee in their shorts. Childhood seemed the devil of a long way off now.

'I've said you're a madman for going down under the sea in a sardine tin, and I'll say it again – and keep on saying it.'

'And, dear cousin, I can say you're a madman for trundling along in a sardine tin on tracks to be shot at by cannons!'

Siegfried digested that, and smiled, and said: 'They tell me you are called Sea Wolves, now, and you have gained the sobriquet of Sea Wolf.'

'So they say.'

'I heard about the loss of your three ace commanders in the space of a week. The news was very cautiously released. I am sorry.'

Wolz could speak with feeling. Prien, Schepke and Kretschmer had, indeed, been aces.

'So am I.'

He did not go on to say that he felt absolutely certain he had witnessed the destruction of U-99, and the sour memories of that night lingered pungently. In addition, Lemp in U-110 must be presumed lost, for nothing had been heard of him or his boat.

The Sea Wolves might be sinking shipping; they were themselves steadily being sunk.

And, in addition, the very concept of thinking of human beings and their ships, men who screamed and died, burned and broiled in a flaming sea, as 'shipping' brought the full horror of the mechanisation and depersonalisation of warfare home to the heart. The war was turning uglier, and judging by what Siegfried had on his mind and was not talking about was likely to get very much worse.

They walked silently back to the schloss where they parted to prepare for the night's high jinks.

# CHAPTER FOUR

'Steer oh-four-five.'

'Steer oh-four-five.'

The night glimmered about them in a ghostly patina of silver over the calm water. A few high clouds patched the glitter of stars with gulfs of emptiness. Only a small breeze blew and that breeze was warm. Ahead lay Italy, and Naples, and, as well as oranges and signorinas and tuneful melodies and spaghetti, a 2-cm flak cannon.

Navy Group South wanted the U-boats under operational command to be fully functional. U-55 would be repaired and receive her new flak gun. Whether or not Wolz would receive a replacement for Wissel remained to be seen. He doubted it.

Co-operation between the Italians and Germans in the anti-shipping war had been uneasy. The Italians now had their own area of the Atlantic in which to operate. But their boats were too large and their methods antique. They had their successes and Wolz wished them well of it. But here in the Med he would be operating under German control, and for that he felt grateful.

'Steady as she goes.'

'Steady as she goes.'

He wouldn't approach too close to the entrances to Naples until daylight, when a minesweeper had been ordered out to escort him in. The Royal Navy had a habit of prowling around and itchy anti-U-boatmen would as lief shoot at him before he could make his identification signals.

The watch kept alert on the bridge, their glasses

clamped to their eyes. The skipper was on the bridge. Woe betide any idiot who fouled up when Baldur Wolz was about.

U-55 slid on across the sea.

Wolz reflected that was just the kind of dumb trick the Kriegsmarine would pull to send him off to the Med just as Rudi von Falkensbach in his U-114 had been attached to the flotilla. Donitz had said he was so desperately short of boats that, with various detachments, he could put only eight or ten boats into the Atlantic.

That was where the most severe and decisive struggle lay. As a U-boatman Wolz knew that. He stared across the smooth water, fitfully lit by the erratic moon, and wondered if all the effort of sending boats into the Med was worth it, even for the sake of Rommel's Afrika Korps. But, his job was to obey orders and sink British ships. The wider strategic issues were not – as yet – his concern.

That did not mean that he, along with everyone else, did not discuss them exhaustively.

The port forrard lookout was relieved and went below.

The Second Watch Officer, Leutnant z. S. Ludwig Riepold, stretched his arms and shifted to a more comfortable position. He had proved to be tough and competent, and, by this time, was the officer who had served longest in U-55. Wolz was not likely to forget that fraught business of picking U-55 up out of a Norwegian fjord.

'Don't make any long-term plans in Naples, Ludwig.'

'No, skipper. I'm saving them up for Malta.'

About to say: 'I wish I had your confidence,' Wolz checked himself.

Instead, he said: 'They say all Italian girls have moustaches.'

'Not true, skipper.'

'So I would hope. There were far too many moustaches

on the French girls – '

'Only a few – '

'Yes. Delightful creatures. But they don't like us.'

'They will. Given time.'

'Time.' Again Wolz checked himself. Time they had had, it seemed, all the time in the world. England was struggling in the toils and must eventually have succumbed. And, now . . .

His dark thoughts went with Siegfried and Manfred as they fought in panzer and Messerschmitt over the wastes of Russia.

That time the three of them had been on leave together – they'd had a right old time! They'd destroyed the wine cellar. And most of the local girls and those down from Berlin had been essayed, escaladed, rammed and boarded, dive-bombed – the schloss hadn't had a quiet minute for days on end.

Dawn was not too far off, and Ehrenberger would come up to take his watch at four. They'd see U-55 picked up by the minesweeper and escorted into Naples –

The starboard forward lookout stiffened. Even before he spoke Wolz was looking out in the direction his glasses followed.

Yes! A shape out there, dark and low and, somehow, ominous.

The lookout reported dubiously.

'Ship bearing green twenty . . .'

Wolz stared hungrily.

Probably that was a Neapolitan ship, a small fishing craft, a coaster, slipping in under the cover of the fading darkness. One thing was sure. That shadow was not a fat English freighter waiting to be sent to the bottom.

'Steady as you go.'

He watched, estimating the course and speed of the other ship. It was hard to see. The moon was little over the quarter and it chose just then to edge out from a cloud. A silver light spread for a moment across the sea.

Wolz gripped his glasses with a convulsion of energy, an abrupt and shaking sense of destiny.

He recognised the conning tower.

He recognised it instantly.

The U-boat out there was not a U-boat.

It was an English submarine.

And she was sailing almost broadside-on to U-55, passing from starboard to port, and without having to make a single course correction, Wolz could bring his four forward tubes to bear.

Quietly, he said: 'Action stations. Prepare tubes one, two, three and four. Hold her steady. This one we will have before breakfast!'

Ginger Everton was feeling miffed because Taffy Owens had scooped the pool and Ginger, although he couldn't prove a thing, fancied the cards weren't all they might have been. Now he stood on the bridge and stared out over the Med and tried to keep his mind on the sea and the confusing shifting patterns of shadow and moonlight.

HM Submarine *Unscathed* stole along in the furtive manner of a thief who has tried a door and found it securely locked. This patrol looked to Ginger as though, on the following night, it would turn out full of highly unpleasant incident.

The skipper, Lieutenant-Commander Ray Bradbury, DSC, a jovial, well-proportioned, highly-coloured young man, was a holy terror when it came to anything to do with submarines. Not a single thing in a tincan escaped his eye. And he was genial with it, too, stripping you off layer by layer until all the flesh was gone and you stood there in your naked bones.

The sea glimmered, smooth and with a long sighing motion that was disturbed only where *Unscathed*'s bow cut a path.

Sub-Lieutenant Pocock, all bum-fluff and pink ears, was

OOW and Ginger fancied he'd have no trouble from him.

*Unscathed* had carried out enough patrols by now for the routines to become established. Ginger looked forward to getting off watch and down into the fore ends and seeing about a cup of kai and then getting his head down in real earnest.

He checked his quadrant again, running the glasses carefully over the sea and the shadows, trying to discern whatever might be out there. The shadows were tricky. The quarter moon kept vanishing into a scattering of cloud and then jumping out again to light up the scene for a few heartbeats before being obliterated again.

The breeze was warm, which was a mixed blessing, and the smells were not too bad. Thank God they did short patrols. What those sods of Jerries had to put up with in their U-boats or even our own chaps out East — well, Ginger Everton had no wish to explore those dismal possibilities.

Taffy Owens down in the asdic cabinet had the Men of Harlech running in and out of his head like dolphins leaping out of the sea and diving cleanly back again. He concentrated on the sounds that were coming in, and together with the tune he was worried that Ginger hadn't taken losing at all well. Ginger hadn't actually accused him of cheating; but he'd come very near. Taffy hadn't been cheating; he was just a better player. All the mess knew that.

A faint susurration came and went on bearing two-oh-five.

Taffy docketted that away and made his one eighty-degree sweep. Back on two-oh-five he paused, listening intently.

He had a good ear. Fine voice, bach, they'd said back in the village choir. But he'd never gone on with the singing. Work had precluded that, and he was not employed by a firm which encouraged a choir. But he could sing a great note, and hold it, and he could hear – what he was hearing now, a muffled shush-shush-shush, vibrated through his ears and into his head and was sorted and analysed by that Welsh musical soul.

Into the quiet of the control room he said: 'HE bearing two-oh-five.'

Lieutenant Webb spun about.

'What's that, Owens?'

'HE bearing red-two-oh-five, sir.'

Webb had been thinking that it was about time for the kai to come up, and was preparing to jolly a few memories. He'd far prefer to be back in Malta, for what that was worth, instead of out here. But they were here and they knew what they were here for. The skipper would have his guts for garters if he fouled up, and, knowing that, Webb checked with Pocock on the bridge.

'Sounds like diesels, sir,' called Taffy Owens. He could hear the HE clearly now. 'Getting closer, sir, about 210 revs.'

'Call the captain.'

All the personnel in the control room were now alive to the situation. They probably had a crafty Eytie coaster up there motoring along and trying to slip into Naples before daylight.

Well, a kipper up his breadbasket ought to settle him.

On the bridge the two lookouts rigidly maintained watch on their sectors, whilst Pocock checked the bearing as it was given to him. It was changing so slowly he recognised that the ship was approaching them on their port beam from the south.

He could see nothing but shadows and the odd glint of star-reflection – the moon was in and out like a yo-yo.

Then, like the Wrath of the Gods, Lieutenant-Commander Ray Bradbury, DSC, was on the bridge at his side. Bradbury might be highly-coloured, well-proportioned; but he had a bristly jaw like the ram of *Iron Duke* and a look in his eyes like the flashing discharge of sixteen-inch guns.

He looked over on the bearing. The moon broke clear.

Ginger Everton, Sub Pocock and the captain all saw the shape fragmentarily revealed, saw the angles, and as one knew what was hissing through the sea at them.

'Dive! Dive! Dive!'

The klaxon exploded into heart-hammering sound.

The lookouts, the sub and the captain went down the hatch in a single co-ordinated rush. Water slapped at Bradbury as he hauled the hatch shut.

Water roared into the Q tanks and *Unscathed* put her head down and dived.

Bradbury was flung against the ladder, and gripped and held on, as his boat plunged recklessly down. He forced himself to drop down into the control room with that calm affection of complete control.

'Eighty feet,' he said. 'Catch a trim first time, Webby.' He smiled. 'I want to go up for a looksee PDQ.'

*Unscathed* plunged below the surface with the white water spouting.


Baldur Wolz said: 'Loose!'

Set to their pre-arranged pattern, four torpedoes left the forward tubes, one after the other, hissing through the water and aimed dead on target.

'We can't miss!' said Ehrenberger from the attack periscope in the tower. 'He's dead to rights!'

'If he doesn't spot us.'

'Counting!'

The seconds ticked away. Wolz felt the thick excitement in his throat. If he could sink an English submarine, that would be a phenomenal beginning to a successful cruise. It would materially assist Rommel, and that was what Wolz was in the Med. to do.

The moon glittered palely, and shadows fleeted and raced away. Tufts of white showed beside the distant target.

Wolz beat his fist on the coaming in fury.

'Go on! Go on!' he shouted, willing the eels to run fast and true.

Those white spouts thickened along the submarine's hull.

Ehrenberger had no need to speak; but he shouted up the pipe in a voice of choked dismay: 'He's diving!'

'You don't expect him to hang about if he's seen us, do you, Kern?'

'No, but . . .!'

'I know –'

The count went on – and went on – and presently Wolz knew he had missed.

'Dive. Flood. Take her down, Chief.'

The lookouts dropped away below and Wolz followed them, trying to be philosophical. Those four expensive torpedoes had hissed through the water above the diving English submarine. They could not have missed by much. At least one might have cracked into a periscope standard. But not one had hit. He slammed the lid and screwed it down and then dropped silently past the steuermann in the tower and landed in the control room.

U-55 went down smoothly enough and already Wolz's head was filled with the computations necessary to outwit the English submarine captain.

No use in hanging around at periscope depth. He would have to dive and then see what the hydrophone operator had to tell him. An underwater duel as such was simply not on, not with the instruments at his disposal. But if the Englishman was incautious, stupid or incompetent . . . From his own experience Wolz knew that the unknown English captain would not be incom-

43

petent. He might be stupid but that, too, was unlikely. But he was quite likely to be incautious. In that case, Wolz might still have him.

The orders were rapped out as required as Wolz checked courses and speeds, tried to think what the enemy would do, held the boat steady, and listened to the reports from the hydrophone operator.

The English submarines were not technically anywhere near as refined as the U-boats. They were rather crude. The capture of *Seal* had shown that. And if that had been a U class, as he felt certain it was, Intelligence indicated that they were very small, coastal craft, inferior to comparable U-boats. But, smallness was an asset in the Med, and she would have four tubes – possibly six – up at the sharp end.

This would be no easy encounter – if it took place.

U-55's Wireless Operator was Willy Marwitz. When submerged the Wireless Operator doubled as the Hydrophone Operator. The acoustic detector fitted in U-55 was highly sensitive and gave off a continuous and monotonous note. Most of the hands would laugh and say the sound had sent Willy off his head. But he was a good ear.

'Nothing, skipper,' reported Marwitz.

The Englishman must be running dead slow on one screw, then.

Wolz conformed.

Both submarines hung in the water, barely creeping along, each listening for the tell-tale sounds of the other.

When it seemed to Wolz that all hope of picking up the enemy had passed he surmised they must have been creeping along on diverging courses.

He gave the order to put about and U-55 cautiously patrolled back. They listened. Willy Marwitz sat with his hands clamped to the headphones over his ears, oblivious to anything but the fishy world outside the pressure hull.

The silence clung to the men in the U-boat, like a second skin.

Wolz wasn't going to go to periscope depth.

The Englishman would be listening out and the sounds of tanks being blown would give away the U-boat and deliver them into the unforgiving jaws of six British torpedoes.

The silence from Willy Marwitz held a different quality from the silence of the rest of the boat.

Wolz refused to keep hovering. No use chivvying Marwitz. When the sounds they all wanted to hear were picked up, then the Wireless Operator would make his report. Until then – wait.

Into his computations he must figure the arrival of the Italian minesweeper. She'd steam up, with the crew no doubt all warbling 'O sole mio', and start fishing around. That could be highly unhealthy for a submerged U-boat.

Cousin Siegfried had not been too sanguine on the alliance with Italy.

'Of course, Baldur, they're good fellows. Charming in their ways.' The two cousins had taken themselves off for a few moments from the racket uproariously bellowing away in the downstairs precincts. With a couple of bottles of champagne they'd gone up to Siegfried's room – 'to recharge batteries, as I'm sure you U-boat fellows would say, Baldur.'

'We would and we do. Here are the glasses. And I have brought an extra bottle.'

Siegfried poured with the skill of long practice.

'I've seen the Italians, Baldur. As I say, charming fellows. But I wouldn't like to serve in any of their panzers. My God! You can put your finger through the plating, it's that thin.'

Wolz nodded.

'Their U-boats are wonderful-looking, but they're ungainly. As allies they leave much to be desired.'

'They're brave enough. It's not their fault that – '

Siegfried stopped talking abruptly as a racket outside the door heralded heavy blows on the polished panels.

He frowned.

'Now what the – ?'

Voices outside lifted in argument. Heated words were being exchanged.

'That sounds like – ' began Wolz.

'Yes. Marlene was due later and she must have arrived sooner than expected.'

Siegfried did not sound too pleased. He sounded less than excited. Wolz decided he would be very very careful. Marlene, who was a well-known entertainer in Berlin, really did care for Siegfried. She used to come down to the schloss and dance in her black SS straps and uniform cap, flaunting her naked body for the delectation of the gathered SS and Gestapo in ways that would have horrified Himmler. She had felt Siegfried slipping away from her and Wolz had done what he could, and that was precious little, to help her. She had appealed to him for assistance.

Wolz told himself he had helped Marlene because he had no wish to become involved with her.

He felt sorry for her, yes, that was true. But she was still beautiful, still superbly made, lush and voluptuous. If she still wanted Siegfried and he was cooling off, she would have to face that. She had everything to draw men to her – if she did not too rapidly ruin herself by drink and smoking and little innocent sniffs.

'Just listen to them!' Siegfried's harsh face betrayed extreme distaste.

In truth, the row outside sounded just like a fish-wives' squabble in a sordid slum-market on the waterfront.

Wolz entertained the dismal suspicion that Marlene had reverted to that brittle, cynical, world-weary guise of the wronged woman, defeated and down. She'd be

46

chain-smoking and drinking heavily again. He'd tried to push this Renate who was after Siegfried off on to Cousin Manfred, and had succeeded for at least one night. But the two women out there screaming shrill obscenities at each other indicated to him that Renate had gone back, or was trying to go back, to her attack on Siegfried.

The situation repelled Wolz. But, and again he did not know why, he felt that little twinge of fellow-feeling for Marlene.

Siegfried, his champagne glass in one hand slopping, crossed swiftly to the door and wrenched it open.

'Don't stand like a couple of bitches in heat out there,' he said unpleasantly. 'You'd better come in. Now!'

The two women entered and Siegfried's room at once became overcrowded, highly-coloured and exotically- perfumed.

The instant Marlene and Renate were in the room and Siegfried had slammed the door they tore into each other.

Renate was not built like a snake, as Marlene so contemptuously dismissed her; but she was slender and lissom and swift-moving, like a cat. She was dressed in normal outdoor clothes, and she leaped at Marlene, seized her hair and tried to drag the taller woman's head down. Marlene screamed and seized Renate's hair. They wrestled and fought across the floor, stumbling over a chair and crashing full-length.

Silk-stocking clad legs thrashed, gleaming in the lights. The stockings were laddered and ruined. Renate shifted her grip and ripped Marlene's blouse down, the white cambric tearing with a loud noise. The women were gasping and panting, screaming, pulling and tugging, clawing.

'Stop that!' shouted Siegfried.

He stepped forward to try to part the wild-cat women and received a long claw-scratch down his face.

He stepped back. He was shaking. His face betrayed his intense fury. Wolz saw that his cousin was disgusted by this display.

The women rolled on the floor, over and over. Now Renate's skirt was torn away, and her slip tangled. She tried to rake Marlene's eyes out. Wolz stepped forward. Enough was enough.

What the women were shrieking at each other was quite incomprehensible. The words were nothings. But the meanings were perfectly plain. Both women were fighting over a single man – and that man was Siegfried.

Wolz got his fingers into Renate's jacket and heaved her back.

'Siegfried – grab Marlene. They'll hurt each other in a minute.'

'Let them –'

'Come on, cousin!'

'Let go you fool!' panted Renate. She twisted her head and tried to bite Wolz.

Calmly, he pushed her head back, keeping his grip on her jacket. She tried to kick him. He moved sideways, still gripping her jacket. With an eel-like wriggle she slid the jacket off. Wolz stood like an idiot holding the jacket as Renate leaped forward at Marlene.

The next few moments were filled with swirling hair and lashing limbs. The women ripped each other's clothes off. They did this with a kind of frenzy of application, as though they had reverted to a primeval barbarism. The ferocity of their mutual hatred chilled Wolz.

'Siegfried – we must stop them. Get hold of Marlene, for God's sake!'

'Very well.'

The SS officer knew how to restrain recalcitrant bodies. He took Marlene in a grip and pulled. As he did so, Wolz wrapped both arms around Renate's slender waist and heaved her back. She came up off the floor, her arms and legs striking out, her hair flying, screaming.

And Marlene, scraps of clothing tangled around her body, seeing who held her, meekly complied, and sagged back against Siegfried and wrapped her arms around his neck, and clung on.

'Oh, Siegfried! Why do you do it, why?'

Wolz did not wish to witness any more. He tucked Renate under his arm. She tried to kick him. With a deft twirl that made her gasp, he reversed her under his arm so that he carried her hanging stern first.

His free hand lifted, opened, came down with a meaty thwack. Her naked buttock abruptly showed the pink imprint of his hand.

'Lie still, girl.'

'You – you – I'll – '

'You'll lie still.'

He crossed to the door. He stopped, looked back.

'Make it up with Marlene, cousin. I'll take care of this she-cat.'

'But – '

Wolz gave Siegfried no time to work out what had happened. He opened the door and went out, holding the half-naked form of Renate firmly. He gave her another slap, just to remind her.

Facing backwards, she could reach down with her hands. She gripped into the back of his thigh with one hand and thrust the other past his other leg. He twisted himself away a little, felt that grasping hand, and said: 'Let go, Renate. That is private property.'

'I know what to do with private property – '

She reached again, and this time Wolz slapped her bottom hard enough to make her squeal.

'I mean it, Renate. Hold still.'

Along the corridor walked a tall woman, immaculately dressed in a long evening gown of shimmering silver. Her hair was mousy in colour, but coiled and coiffed, and

49

her make-up was over-bright. She had a gleam in her eye. She was towing an SS-Hauptsturmführer. He was being hauled along in a dishevelled uniform with his shirt hanging out. He saw Wolz with the half-naked woman under his arm and the pink hand-shaped splotches on her buttocks.

'That's the way,' cried the SS-Hauptsturmführer. 'Up the Sabines, say I – '

'You'll be up who and what I say, Dodi, and don't you forget it.'

The regal-looking woman gave him an impetuous pull and he went staggering off after her, his two-inch heels only barely making contact with the carpet. Wolz had to laugh.

Amazingly, Renate laughed, echoing Wolz.

'That Gretchen! She likes little men. She eats 'em.'

'So you've come to your senses, Renate. Good.'

Wolz pushed open the door to Manfred's room with its aeroplane models and splintered propeller and all the things of his consuming interest that paralleled the things of Siegfried's consuming interests in his brother's room. Each to his own, and each room was a portrait of its occupant.

'You'll have to wait here until you're in a fit state – '

'I'm fit now, Baldur! You shouldn't have smacked me – it hurt – '

'If you could have seen yourself you'd thank me.'

'Not for that bitch Marlene.'

'She's all right – '

'Oh, no! She's got no rights to Siegfried – it's open season where he's concerned.'

'Do you go after everything in trousers?'

'No. I'm particular.' She stared at him. She was not in the slightest bothered over her appearance, the fact that her slip and brassiere hung around her waist, that her breasts trembled as she walked across to the bed and flung herself down. Wolz muted the lights to the standard lamp and put his hand on the door knob.

'Where d'you think you're going, Baldur?'

He was going to find Manfred. He would not tell her that.

'Give you time to cool off.'

'I'm hot, Baldur.' She held out one arm. It was a nice gesture. It indicated desire and invitation; but it was calculated. She did not lift both arms, that would have been *de trop*.

'Yes. Cool off.'

'No. Baldur, you fool – look at me!'

'Very nice.'

'You beast!'

'Yes. I'm going to lock the door. If you shout I'll say you've drunk too much and are dangerous – '

She picked up the book on the bedside table and threw it.

Wolz did not bother to duck. His eye had seen instantly that the trajectory would take the book to thud against the light switch. He smiled at her.

'Just take what you have, Renate. Poaching and poachers are frowned on around here.'

'It's nothing to do with you! I'll – '

She leaped off the bed and started for him. Wolz did not like the look in her eyes. He opened the door and ducked out. He slammed it and locked it only just in time.

Thoughtfully, he dropped the key in his pocket.

Then he went off to find Manfred and give him the key to his own room and warn him of the sexual bombshell he would find locked up inside.

The impression remained of that long, red, shining scratch on the upper surface of Renate's left breast.

The fullness of her figure and the snake-like way she moved created a profound impression.

Wolz shook his head. He was sharp set for a girl, well enough, a not unusual condition for healthy young men, and yet for Renate he could feel nothing of the depth of feeling he felt for Lottie or Heidi in their romps. Even Marlene, for all her silly excesses that ravaged her, held more meaning for Baldur Wolz.

Life was a funny old business.

As U-55 nosed on towards Naples, Wolz reflected that if he was no better at handling a U-boat than he was at handling women, they were in for a rough cruise.

On sour thoughts that perhaps he ought to have taken a trim at periscope depth and listened out for the Englishman there, instead of taking the safer course, he brought U-55 in towards the rendezvous with the Italian minesweeper. Better safe than sorry. There were precious few second chances in a U-boat. And Baldur Wolz's plans for the Mediterranean did not include getting his boat and himself sunk.

# CHAPTER FIVE

Naples proved to be a complete fiasco for the men of U-55. With German thoroughness a naval shore party was waiting for them. The twisted rails of the winter-garden could be re-twisted back into shape, the holes patched. The smashed 2-cm was removed and the new one, brought specially all the way down Italy, installed. The men of U-55 watched all this hectic work glumly.

As Mueller put it: 'We're now immortal – according to my English teacher back home in Flensburg.'

'How's that, Mueller, you old hermit-crab?'

Mueller was one of the elektro-machinists. He waved his arms at what could be seen of the city – the duomo, the narrow cramped roofs, the prospect out towards the Vesuvius, not even to the Castle of the Egg. Walls surrounded them and reflected the sunshine and the clang of hammers, the hiss of welders.

'I'll tell you why we're immortal,' he said in a most disgruntled tone. ' "See Naples and Die." That's a saying they have – it's a joke on the island's name. Well, we've never seen Naples, have we, so we won't die, will we?'

They shouted at him and then Riepold appeared and the hands bent to their tasks again.

But at the thought of all those ripe young signorinas and all that beautiful vino just across there – well, it made you want to spit.

U-55 sailed in the late afternoon, and Wolz kept her on the surface to make a good run eastwards after he'd rounded the toe and heel of the peninsula.

A further series of reports had come in about the

English submarine lurking in the approaches, and the minesweeper fellows of the Italian Navy claimed to have driven the submarine off. They did not – and Wolz was intrigued to note this – they did not claim to have sunk her.

He was relying on the reports' accuracy.

If the damned Englishman was hanging about in the offing, he'd certainly have a crack at U-55.

But the port commander had assured Wolz that there was now no danger whatsoever.

All the same, Wolz did not leave his bridge.

Marwitz sat clamped to his equipment, a part of it, the human part with the brain and the ear. What sounds came vibrating through the water had to be listened to and analysed and decided on. Marwitz was well aware of the vital importance of his job in the boat.

With the coming of full daylight they were well on their way and safely free of the possible lurking areas of the English submarines. Wolz yawned. He'd been on the bridge for the major part of sixteen hours or so. That was no novelty, of course; but he wanted to store up his sleep as much as possible for the fraught times ahead. He could leave the deck in the capable hands of his Watch-Keeping Officers. By this time they could read what the different upward slants of that evil black cigar that jutted from the corner of their skipper's mouth could mean in various situations.

'Keep her as she goes, Kern. And keep an eye on those two midshipmen. I want their noses ground into the work. I don't want another Otto von Magdorf – '

Ehrenberger looked suitably horrified.

'Amen to that, skipper!'

'Right. Call me if – you know.'

'Very good.'

As he dropped down the ladder into the control room, Wolz reflected that you tended to run through shipmates in the U-boat arm. Again and again he congratulated himself on retaining his cadre of experienced officers. He'd had some nasty blots sailing with him before. And Leutnant Freyer, for all his confounded Wagner, was shaping up.

Mind you, as Wolz went through the control room with an intolerant eye out for any irregularity in the shine of switches and the maze of pipes and levers, mind you, he quite liked Wagner – every so often.

Even Richard Strauss was capable of offering good things. Nothing like the real Strausses, though, nothing like at all.

He lay on his bunk and then Fahnrich Friedrich Thumen was shaking his shoulder.

'First Officer, sir – would you come to the bridge – '

Wolz brushed past the midshipman before he had framed a reply. He was hurtling into the wardroom when he heard the shouts.

'Flood! Dive!'

The thumping rattle of the diesels died at the exact right moment as the Chief cut them off the instant the boat dived, switching in the electric motors. The air pressure barely altered. Only the slightest of ear-pops betrayed any difference. Water splashed down from the hatch, and the lookouts dropped on to the deck and dived out of the way of the next man down.

Ehrenberger dropped down last, shutting off the hatch. He saw Wolz.

'A Swordfish, skipper – '

'Right. Course, speed, bearing?'

The boat was on the way down.

In the North Sea or the Atlantic it would have been perfectly proper to have stayed at periscope depth. He could have had a good look around through the sky search scope.

But here in the Mediterranean that was asking for trouble.

The clarity of the water would mean the pilot and

observers in the Swordfish could see his betraying bulk beneath the surface. They'd fly over him and drop a depth charge down at their leisure.

Ehrenberger rattled off the details.

Wolz bent over the chart table under the blue light. 'H'm. You've brought us a long way south, Kern.'

'Yes.'

Wolz looked up.

At his skipper's expression, Ehrenberger explained.

'Orders, skipper. We were re-routed on to this course just after midday. I didn't wake you – '

'No.'

Ehrenberger looked mutinous.

Well, Wolz decided, his Number One was protecting the skipper from petty interruptions that would have destroyed the sleep he needed. And a straightforward course alteration was just that – straight forward.

'No reason given?'

'No, skipper.'

'Well, we'll check when we make radio contact next.'

'Very good.'

All their lives hung on invisible threads. The radio gave them orders, and encouragement and advice. Through the air they felt in contact with their own.

A mistake would mean the end for all of them. These thoughts added up to that essential feeling of the U-boat arm as being special, a band of brothers, dedicated to fighting the war at sea in the only way they knew.

After Wolz had seen U-55 safely through the Strait of Messina he had expected their course to head up to the north-east. Naval Group South had ordered them south of that course and the reason could only be Malta. The English must be attempting to run a convoy through, and U-55 was being lined up for the attack. As soon as the first boat contacted the convoy the sighting would be transmitted and the pack would home in.

Wolz felt the beginning of that old familiar tremble of excitement.

Ehrenberger caught that feeling, too.

'Malta, skipper. I felt it – '

Riepold appeared, rubbing his eyes, his hair in a mess. He was dressed like them all in a sloppy rig that was comfortable and practical. Wolz demanded effort and absolute efficiency. The rig his men wore was dictated by those demands.

'Malta?' said Riepold. 'That's as bad as Gibraltar.'

'If we get in among a convoy – ' said Ehrenberger.

'If they find it,' Wolz pointed out.

'We'll notch up some more tonnage!'

There was no repressing these fire-eaters.

U-55 continued on course. The LI reported all systems functioning correctly. That was a pleasant fact to record.

Tactfully, Ehrenberger made the suggestion Wolz knew he would make.

'We'll have to stay down for a bit, skipper. Our batteries are on full charge – why don't you – ?' He stopped, and looked away. Even with the friendly comradeship that had developed between the officers of U-55, the IWO ventured to give his commander suggestions at his own peril.

'Right, Kern. I'll get my head down. Wake me in one hour. Even a Swordfish has to go home to roost.'

'Very good!'

But, this time, sleep eluded Baldur Wolz.

He had the Mediterranean to play in. But all seas are governed by the trade routes. The British were desperately trying to run supplies into Malta. The Luftwaffe was knocking hell out of the island. But the supplies were the key. Wolz did not have the whole of the inland sea to play in. He had to go where the pickings were – and that meant going in among the English destroyers.

Well, he'd done that before and he'd do it again. It was not a nice thought. But he'd do it.

This time he did not get off to sleep as easily as he had the last time. His mind's eye was filled with the ghastly roar of exploding tankers, of men burning in the burning sea. And, mixed in with these uneasy visions as he twisted uneasily on his bunk the image of Renate, half-naked, with that scratch vivid and red on her breast, tormented him. Well, as he was fond of saying, he knew what he wanted out of life and he intended to take it.

Trouble was, he really was not at all sure just what it was he did want. He had thought, Cousin Lisl being beyond his dreams, that he would ask Trudi von Hartstein to marry him. He had thought she would say yes. And then she had been attacked mysteriously in a German wood by machine-pistol armed men and her friends killed. And then she had demanded he drive her to the Bodensee, and seen him off, without saying a real goodbye.

Now what had happened to her?

What, come to that, was happening in Germany?

He did not know.

He heard snatches of gossip, incautious drunken remarks that did not make sense. Perhaps, one day, he would find out. As a mere Oberleutnant zur See he was so low in the scale his existence was of no importance to anyone but himself.

Take that party where Marlene and Renate had had their screaming scratching fight.

He'd gone back to the main room of the schloss where the four enormous fireplaces were filled with country flowers. There he'd been buttonholed by the Herr Professor Dentz.

'Ah! Our gallant U-boat commander!'

Wolz stared at the Herr Professor. The man looked like

a penguin and Wolz realised he meant nothing offensive in the remark. Quite the reverse. Dentz knew about U-boats.

'You have had good hunting since our last meeting, Herr Wolz?'

Wolz nodded.

'Not as good as I could hope for. But you are aware of the handicaps under which we U-boat people have to fight the war.'

'Indeed, yes.'

Dentz was plump, bespectacled, sweating just a little, his chubby face creased into smiles. But those ice-chip eyes and the thin tightness to the lips indicated that there was far more to Herr Professor Dentz than appeared to anyone who might mistakenly regard him as a plump genial penguin kind of fellow.

Wolz salvaged a glass and a bottle of champagne from a small side table which was in imminent danger of being knocked flying by the silk-stocking clad legs of a young lady whose chemise rode higher with every lunge. Her companion on the couch was roaring a drunken song. He looked flushed and happy and without tunic or trousers his white shirt might belong to anyone.

'You will be happy to know, Herr Wolz, that what I indicated to you as being promising developments in the U-boat research programme are now coming along very nicely. Naturally, I cannot say anything specific. But it is my view that the men in the boats should be told that good days are coming.'

'Provided we live long enough.'

'Yes. Of course.' Dentz extended his glass and Wolz filled it. 'Tell me. You still command a Type VIIB?'

'Yes.'

'They are now so old-fashioned it is beyond belief. The only consolation we have is that the English boats are even more old-fashioned.'

'I tend to attack surface ships —'

'But of course! I was merely making the comparison. The Type VIIC is a much better boat. But we will have to fight the war with them until — well, until the better days are here.'

'I flew in a Kondor with the Luftwaffe to have a look at their side of the operations whilst my boat was being repaired. I have to say I was not impressed by what has been accomplished. But —'

'But you would be wise not to say so, hein?'

'Precisely.'

Despite the dangers inherent in the situation, Wolz felt he could fashion some kind of relationship with this peculiar scientific gentleman.

And then, as they talked around the subject, with Wolz continually tantalised by the hints thrown out of better boats to come, an SS-Standartenführer lurched by. He was quite clearly drunk. His face, heavy, wrinkled, was flushed to a plum colour, and he thrust his chin forward as though by main force alone he would remain upright. He clutched to the arm of a little man in a plain civilian coat whose white face was pinched, whose eyes possessed the grey chill of a Norwegian fjord, and whose mouth looked as though it had not forgotten how to smile but had never had that knowledge.

'We're going to — going to put things on a — proper basis,' hiccoughed the SS-Standartenführer.

He almost fell over the sprawled legs of the white-shirted man on the couch whose drunken song had burbled away to a silly rumple-tumple-te-tum. The girl on the couch was giggling and pushing her chemise down every time it rode up.

The SS-Standartenführer regarded the two on the couch with a loose and unfocussed smile.

'Action stations all the way. That's the SS!'

'Of course, Heinrich,' said the white-faced civilian. He

wore gold-rimmed glasses. They glinted coldly. 'But—'

'Got it all worked out.'

The SS-Standartenführer—chuckling and shaking his head—reached down over the shoulder of the man on the couch and tweaked at the girl. She did not scream. But she gave a surprised little gasp and her hands left the chemise, which immediately lifted like a sail in a breeze. She rubbed her breast and stared indignantly up at the SS officer.

He chuckled and then staggered three paces to leeward and only the support of his companion saved him from going head over heels across a chair lying on its side.

'Yes,' he said, as he lurched back. 'All you do is drop the little pellets. Lovely. Clean, efficient, neat. The right German way—'

'Please come along, Heinrich—'

'Got a lot to thank—to thank you scientific fellows for, Herr Doktor. What we SS—SS need. Zyklon-B. That's the stuff—that's the stuff—'

'SS-Standartenführer!'

The shrivelled little civilian spoke in a voice that shocked through the hubbub, penetrating this corner of the room, cutting like a rambow through ice.

He looked meaningfully into the SS man's bloodshot eyes as he spoke in that scathing voice.

'One more word—one more! And you are reported—'

'No, no, Herr Doktor. You know me! I love my work—all of you know that!'

'Come along then—and leave that girl alone. I want you to meet—'

The two shambled off, the little civilian leading the lurching SS-Standartenführer like a fussy tug leads a stricken battlecruiser out of action.

Wolz shook his head.

Herr Professor Dentz regarded Wolz.

'Herr Oberleutnant. A word of advice. A friendly word.

You heard nothing.'

Wolz did not laugh. He drew one eyebrow down.

'It's not that I heard nothing, Herr Professor. It's that anything I did hear meant nothing to me. No sense at all.'

Dentz suddenly slumped and put a hand to his side.

'You are all right – ?'

'Yes, yes, thank you. It's just that nothing really does make any sense any more.'

Wolz had to fall back on rote.

'Only the war, duty and my job. What else is there?'

'I think, Baldur – may I call you Baldur? – I think,' and here the Herr Professor Dentz spoke with a sombre emphasis that brought Wolz's senses quiveringly alert. 'That they will not prove enough, not prove anywhere near enough, in the fullness of time.'

'I do not – ?'

'No. I need another drink.'

Wolz piloted the Herr Professor through the next hour by the simple process of ensuring that the penguin-man's glass was never empty.

'Y'know, Baldur – I may call you Baldur? – I just want to put the finest weapons I can contrive into the hands of our brave boys and win the war. Then I can go back to my real work.'

'Oh?'

'Yes, real work.' The glass was emptied and refuelled.

'Can you – ?'

'Of course. It is fash – fasht – wonderful.'

Wolz decided that the next emptying of the Herr Professor's glass had best be the last. He'd help the old penguin to bed and then see about bed himself. That thought cheered him up.

'Y'know Drager make the escape appa – apra – devices?'

'Lungs to get out of a sunken boat. Yes.'

'I plan to equip men to breathe under the sea like they do on land. Baldur – I may call you Baldur? – it is poshible and it will work. Thash what I want to do with my life.'

When Wolz assisted the Herr Professor up to the room allocated to him along the rather too-dusty corridors of old and deeply-polished panelled walls, the penguin was mumbling about his bootiful Zaunkonig and the boats they were going to get from Ingenieursburo Gluck-auf. Wolz soothed him, aware that the bureau had planned some monsters that from his own experience were too big and too out of date. They found the right bedroom and Wolz dropped the Herr Professor on to the bed. Then, with a little smile, he put him to bed properly.

Then, Wolz upped his spargel and went a-hunting.

The craft he spied and chased and eventually boarded proved to be sweet and rounded and scented and cuddly and Wolz fired off his forward torpedoes in fine style. But, all the same, as he staggered off to his own room with his jacket slung over his shoulders, still and all, it wasn't the same.

What he wanted he was not sure; he wanted to get to sea to sink ships so that he might not have to go to sea to sink any more ships again, ever . . .

As for the gibberish the SS-Standartenführer had been spouting, that meant nothing to him.

Manfred, his Luftwaffe uniform dishevelled, staggered into sight along the corridor. He was smiling foolishly.

'Hi, Cousin! You were right. A bombshell.'

So that was all right.

'Goodnight, Manfred. Time for touchdown.'

'Goodnight. Time to dive.'

Somehow or other, towards five in the morning, a semblance of peace and quietness descended on the schloss.

And now, here he was, waiting for the sighting signal to come in vectoring U-55 on to the Malta convoy.

He wished he had some of the wonder-boats the penguin-professor had been promising.

The sizzle of sparks warned him. Number One had the bridge. Wolz waited by the wireless compartment.

Marwitz listened and scribbled and then handed the signal across. Wolz took it and the Enigma went through its paces and he walked carefully to the chart table. He started to work out the course. Over the horizon steamed British ships. And U-55 like a sea-wolf was about to go lethally down among them.

# CHAPTER SIX

'Up periscope.'

'Up periscope.'

Wolz seized the handles and swung the sky search scope in a quick three sixty degree sweep. He steadied for a moment on one-seven-five, took a swift but careful look.

'Down periscope.'

'Down periscope.'

With a hiss the asparagus slid down into its well.

Wolz looked at his officers.

'Smoke. A fair amount – so that means merchantmen. Any more from U-331?'

Marwitz reported that nothing more had been heard from the sighting boat.

Von Thiesenhausen in U-331 was a fine officer, and Wolz was looking forward confidently to adding to his tonnages of ships sunk. Guggenberger in U-81 was also present. U-boats were in desperately short supply, and BdU wanted them in the Atlantic. But in the Med they were, and must make their mark there.

'Steer two-seven-oh.'

'Steer two-seven-oh.'

Wolz put U-55 on a course due west, for the moment content to parallel that betraying cloud of smoke. The difficulty besetting any U-boat commander was the nicety of judging the onset of dusk and sunset. He had to pace the convoy ready to attack. But if he was too cautious and maintained too great a distance he would easily lose sight of the target.

If he was bold and closed in too early he could easily be spotted by the escorts, or one of the patrolling aircraft if a carrier was present. That was a recipe for disaster.

Wolz held on, taking occasional observations, coming to the surface as the darkness deepened to pick up speed and take a more southerly course.

He stared fretfully through the glasses. Now he could make out the loom of ships. They appeared to him vague and lumpy, mere splodges of a darker darkness.

Someone was chattering on the wireless. Wolz maintained silence, listening out, watching the ships, watching the last lingering radiance in the western sky.

When, at last, he gave the order to swing south, he fancied he was putting his head into the lion's jaws. The mangy British lion was reputed to have moth-eaten fur and rotten teeth. But he knew he could still bite.

One of the lumps of shadow was appreciably darker and more pronounced than the others. There was a streak of white at the base of that dark shadow.

Wolz frowned.

Ehrenberger said: 'He can't possibly have spotted us.'

'No.'

But the ominous shape bore on. The bone in the teeth of the onrushing warship strengthened.

'Can't or not, Number One. He has!'

'But –'

'Clear the bridge. Flood. Dive!'

Wolz was the last down. He took a quick look around before he slammed the lid. The darkness was now of that opaque luminous Mediterranean variety so deadly for U-boats.

The hatch clanged over his head and his face was wet.

The destroyer couldn't have spotted them, surely? Not at that range, not in those visibility conditions? But he had swung out from the screen and come haring straight for them almost as though he could see them as though it was broad daylight.

U-55 dived deep.

Presently they heard that ghastly thrashing of screws over their heads.

The sound reverberated down through the water and echoed in the pressure hull. The vroom-vroom echoed in their skulls, too. That sound alone had made many a man break.

Wolz stood in his control room and looked at his men. They all stood with their heads half-inclined, waiting.

'Quarter speed on port motor.'

U-55 eased along, turning away from the vector line. If Wolz could escape immediate detection from the destroyer's asdic he could fool her. If he was picked up . . .

The sounds of the destroyer's screws changed in pitch. They faded. Then they returned, louder than before. Everyone stood as though graven from rock.

The thrashing noise like a train bursting from a tunnel smashed down. Then – mercifully – it faded, hovered as though uncertain, and, presently, died away.

Wolz let out a deep breath.

'We breathe again. Take her up to periscope depth, Chief.'

'Very good!'

When Wolz looked again at the night-shrouded sea he wanted to break one of his own cast-iron rules and curse like a bargee.

The convoy had taken a fresh course, part of its zig-zag. Now, as he stared in appalled fascination, he saw the armada of ships bearing down on him. On their present course the convoy and the U-boat would meet, fatefully.

He felt that the gods had delivered the English into his hands.

But the slightest slip now would mean inevitable destruction.

At periscope depth he watched, his brain alive with the calculations. He would have to allow for the angle without lengthy manoeuvring. A ship was going to pass before him and he was going to loose his four eels.

Afterwards, that, if he got away, would be the time to shout.


Alf Henson was a member of the card school the mess had dubbed The Four Aces. Now he polished up the brass work in the engine-room with an oily rag. He might only be an HO rating; but he liked engines. He was proud to serve in HMS *Melpomene*.

'*Melpomene?*' A scrub-faced young whipper-snapper had said in a bar in Pompey. 'Oh, I see. That makes you all a bunch of lyres – '

He'd not got any further.

Charlie Hattersall, as big around the gut as he was across the shoulders, had crowned him with his beer glass, yelling: 'Liars! I'll give you liars, you – '

The fight had been interesting.

Later on, Alf Henson discovered that the runt had been half-educated at some posh school and was referring to some muse or other who was in charge of tragedy and lyres.

'A lyre, that's like a defunct violin, Alf,' Bert Swanson told him, laughing.

'Well, he got what he asked for, didn't he?'

But they were all proud of *Melpomene*. She was a *Dido*. She displaced five thousand four hundred and fifty tons and she was a sleek five hundred and twelve feet long by a mere fifty and a half beam. With her four screws being urged by sixty-two thousand horsepower turbines she could really turn on the knots. Alf knew she could do better than the figure they always quoted –

thirty-three knots. She was a high-strutting, high-stepping fancy cruiser, *Melpomene*, and her crew put up with her somewhat cramped accommodation because of that.

When they'd had a go at a bunch of Eytie three-engined torpedo bombers the five twin turrets had been spouting like a fireworks display. Three turrets up front. She looked like a buzzsaw when she went into action. Ten 5.25-inch guns she had, dual-purpose. The ammo was a little on the heavy side but they had husky devils in the turrets. Alf would bet if they had to they could shoot down anything that flew.

And they would have to on this dicey run.

'Soon as we get back to Alex –' Fred Dunster started to say to Alf.

Up on the bridge Sub-Lieutenant Guy Hawkins was standing on the starboard side of the bridge, looking out across the darkling sea, and dreaming of getting back to Alice and the wedding. A nice quiet country church, and a country pub, and the best room, and – well, now he was watching *Caerleon* going haring off to the north. She must have picked up something. Give Hawkins the daylight when he could get going with his guns. All this poking about at night with the threat of U-boats and torpedoes was not his idea of the Navy.

All over HMS *Melpomene* the watch on duty did their jobs and thought of pleasures to come, and took comfort from their tiddly ship, and talked of home and girls and what they were going to do. Everyone felt elated at the two Eyties claimed as certainly shot down.

Those Italian torpedo-bomber blokes were really mad. They'd come in low over the sea in their lumbering three-engined buses just asking for it. But they came on and on, and *Melpomene*'s entire gunpower had to be unleashed to discourage them.

The Captain, Aubrey Smithers, DSC, RN, came on to the bridge to stand for a few moments beside the Sub.

Hawkins was aware of the presence at his shoulder.

For a few moments the captain remained silent.

When he did speak he surprised Hawkins.

'How'd you like to be a U-boat commander, Sub, and be swanning around out there now?'

Hawkins said: 'I wouldn't, sir.'

'No more would I. You'd be stuck down there in your tin can figuring the angles, wondering how best to get your kippers in. How'd you do it, then?'

'Well, sir . . .' Hawkins hesitated. Captain Smithers was your smart, efficient, torpedo-like Naval officer, with an eye like a gimlet, who left things to the First Lieutenant and who always knew exactly what was going on in his ship. He'd come from an old falling-to-bits C class cruiser that had been tortured beyond the strength of plates and rivets on the cruel Northern Patrol. He knew cruisers. And, now, Hawkins saw, he was trying to get to know the beastly habits of U-boats. He was trying to make the Sub see what the enemy was thinking.

'I'd be carrying on as usual, sir. The U-boats have been terribly successful with their tactics. They won't change them yet – will they?'

'We'll have to make them.'

'Yes, sir.'

'And we're just a sitting target for these damned U-boat vermin. All our strength will avail us nothing come night fall.'

'We got two aircraft, sir – '

'U-boats, at night, Sub. U-boats.'

'Aye, aye, sir.'

And Captain Aubrey Smithers turned away, back to his permanent position on the bridge. Just a sitting target. That was all his lovely *Melpomene* was at night. But the arrival of the sun would bring SM 79s. Then his ten 5.25s could bite. He loved his new command, with her two raked funnels and her clean lines, and all the gadgetry the Navy had installed to beat the enemy.

Yes, come daylight, and *Melpomene* would once more become a fighting unit. Let the Italians bring on their cruisers, six-inch, eight-inch, they would all be served by *Melpomene*. Even a battleship, given the speed of the *Dido*'s, their agility and smoke-making ability, and the marked reluctance of the Italian Navy to commit its heavy units, might not come amiss, either . . .

A slim, slender, highly lethal light cruiser, HMS *Melpomene*, bristling with guns and ready for action. Britain could do with another twenty like her.

Another slim, lethal shape slid through the warm waters of the Mediterranean.

Wolz brought U-55 along with a precision of judgment that spoke eloquently of the expertise in U-boat handling he had acquired. He was vaguely aware that by this time he had become a master in U-boat warfare; but that was a mere normal part of his daily life at sea. He just could not afford to be anything less.

'Prepare forward tubes.'

The Fahnrich in the fore ends would get stuck in now, Wolz hoped, with a fellow feeling for the boat. Fanatical Nazis had to buckle down to it when a boat went into action like everyone else. If Dietrich Jagow made a mistake there was no easy way out by pleading membership of the party.

He'd created a stupid and unnecessary scene when someone had laughingly referred to the swastika as a *Wolfhandkrabbe*.

'I'll report you! You'll be punished!'

Riepold had had to intervene. The IIWO possessed a hard inner competence Wolz valued, and he'd handled the incident firmly and tactfully. Ehrenberger had passed along the details of the incident and as Wolz read off the courses and bearings, and continually calculated angles came back to him, he reflected that if a U-boat man got upset at the swastika, the symbol of the Nazi party, being called a *Wolfhandkrabbe*, then he was not really cut out to serve in the U-boat arm of the Kriegsmarine.

*Wolfhandkrabbe* was the general nickname in the boats for the swastika, named for an unpleasant-looking fresh-water crab. It had found its way from the Far East and infested European waters, and now its name was the nickname for the swastika.

'Steer one-seven-five.'

'Steer one-seven-five.'

Almost due south, the pointing snout of U-55 lowered four tubes upon the enemy.

'Bow caps open.'

Wolz nodded. U-55 was ready. He put up the periscope in mere fragments of time. It seemed to Ehrenberger not least more than a miracle that the skipper could see so much and understand so much with so short periods of observation.

Kern Ehrenberger knew that was what being a superb U-boat commander meant. Baldur Wolz, with his fierce black cigar, unlit, jutting up from the corner of his mouth, was a superb U-boat commander.

That thought gave Ehrenberger deep comfort. They were going into action and he wouldn't want to go into danger and depth-charging and traumatic psychological pressures with anyone better than Baldur Wolz.

'Up periscope.'

Almost before Wolz had his eye to the tube and looked he was giving the order: 'Down periscope.'

'Angles?'

The attack table spewed out the answers to the calculations. Wolz listened as they were relayed.

He sat on the saddle seat of the attack periscope in the tower and he pondered. That convoy was going far too fast. He was used to the lumbering six or seven knots flocks of sheep of the Atlantic. If they reached eight knots they were pumping huge clouds of smoke into the atmosphere, betraying them for miles. But this little lot were fairly licking along.

'Steer one-eight-five.'

'Steer one-eight-five.'

He was closing in and he must forereach on them. The outer screen had been passed and he had seen no further signs of that nosey destroyer.

'Up periscope.'

This time he concentrated on the shapes steaming along in a flock he intended to rend.

'Down periscope.'

Well, now . . .

There were tankers there, they could not be mistaken. There was also a cruiser rather nearer to him than he had expected. Any destroyers ought to be astern . . . Ought to be.

He took another swift observation, the scope going up and down in moments.

Yes . . . There was that destroyer, foaming along over two thousand metres away astern. He ought to be outside the range of her underwater detection apparatus. Again, there was that ought to be . . .

Another swift look ahead and the final bearings rattled off.

The settings were made. The atmosphere in the boat grew even more tense. They were aware, these men of his, that something different was going on. How they knew he'd never know. He was stuck up in the conning tower at the attack periscope and they were at their stations in the pressure hull; but they knew, they knew . . .

The time was almost here . . .

Wolz took an observation he intended should be the last.

73

What he saw made him grip on to the handles with a ferocity that shook him with its sudden revelation of how much of him was wrapped-up in this attack. He had been so calm and collected, and now, now he saw everything sliding away and fading, the hope gone.

The convoy had altered course. They were going on to the zag leg of their eternal zig-zag.

The cruiser's silhouette passed before him.

Yes – if the convoy was lost to him for now, the cruiser was not. He saw the two raked funnels, the sleek lines of her, vaguely as though seen through a mist.

If he was to shoot he must shoot now. Everything was in his favour – but only for the cruiser.

Four torpedoes for one cruiser?

That seemed a useful profit for the Fatherland.

'Stand by!'

The attack table had done its work. He had done his work. Now everything lay in the inscrutable lap of the gods of chance . . .

'Loose!'

In order, one, two, three, four, the eels left their tubes. Loeffler flooded up to compensate, and U-55 barely bucked.

The hiss of escaping air sounded like the long-drawn sigh of a dying man.

They waited. They counted, stopwatch in hand, or counting on their fingers, or counting in their heads.

'Torpedoes running!'

'Very good.'

Time – against sound advice but necessary now – for a single last-minute flashing observation of the destroyer.

She raced on, astern, aloof to the doings of the U-boat inside her protective screen.

They waited and they counted . . .

Wolz could feel his heart beating. A thick choking sensation blocked his throat.

They counted . . .

No good . . . The count had reached the penultimate second . . . They must have missed . . . The last second ticked away . . .

Missed . . .

Two deep thuds reverberated through the water.

Marwitz let out an exultant yell.

'We got him!'

Two hits out of four . . . Wolz felt the sudden tremble deep in the pit of his stomach.

Two eels striking a light cruiser . . .

'Take us down, Chief. Eighty metres.'

U-55, a lethal steel shark, dived deep . . .

# CHAPTER SEVEN

HMS *Melpomene* was a spanking brand new light cruiser.

Her armour plate measured two inches in thickness, here and there. Her bottom was tinfoil.

Two torpedoes struck her.

She was kippered in the starboard engine-room.

She was kippered aft, and the explosion ripped up the flats and tore off the stern section, the two 5.25-inch turrets slipping and toppling into the water with the wreckage.

Alf Henson and the rest of the card school called The Four Aces died instantly.

No one had a chance of survival aft.

Sub-Lieutenant Hawkins on the bridge felt the shocks heavy and frightening, and the sudden dead feeling of the ship.

Steam lines fractured and high-pressure steam hissed maddeningly. Men screamed as the steam broiled them alive.

Wreckage began to crumple under the impact of the sea in what was now the after sections. *Melpomene*, it was thought, had not much longer to live.

The sea poured ravenously into the engine rooms.

The aft bulkhead had taken a battering and, weakened by the blast, gave way.

The sea poured on.

Aubrey Smithers picked himself up. He shook his shoulders and settled his duffle coat. He knew what the situation was and what the only order left to him to give was.

But it was hard, damned hard.

'Abandon ship,' said the captain.

Men were already going over the side. The darkness was made lurid by the fires bursting up from the cruiser's midships. The constant clanging and banging muddled men's thoughts. But discipline held. The First Lieutenant had been blown to pieces; but the other officers who survived held on to their training. Of traditions only the regular hardcase navy men could call on them. But the HO men rallied. Carley rafts were cut adrift. The water was warm enough so that men might live long enough to be picked up.

The bridge personnel waited for the captain.

'You heard my order, gentlemen.'

No good arguing with Smithers. He was Navy.

Sub-Lieutenant Hawkins thought of Alice and the wedding, and he said, braving the wrath he knew would follow: 'You'll jump, sir?'

'Sub?' The word was distant, almost frosty.

In a rush, wondering at himself for being able to speak so foolishly, yet quite unable to stop himself, Hawkins burst out: 'You *will* jump, sir? You won't do anything –anything foolish–'

'*Sub!*'

'Aye, aye, sir.'

Hawkins went to the rail. The ship was well over on her beam ends. It looked an infernal long way down. You could break your back jumping from this high up. He started to look for a rope or an easier way down.

Now they were all gone from the bridge.

Smithers leaned against the screen and saw how ghostly the bridge looked, with all that gleaming modern equipment silent and useless. He had loved *Melpomene*. She was a ship. She had been a ship. Now she was a sinking wreck.

A gust of primeval hatred for the U-boat flamed all

across his brain. He shook with the enormity of his hatred.

Then, slowly, he made his way down the ladder.

No one remained in the fore parts. The after section was long gone. The ship lay over, quietly, heaving with the sea. Smithers went down the ladders and out into the dimness. The triple row of turrets lifted blindly to the sky. Six 5.25-inch guns in twin turrets, one above the other, they mocked him with their uselessness in this situation.

He walked forward.

She was going. The movement of the ship was sluggish and heavy, waterlogged. She was not even a whole ship any more.

Quietly, Captain Aubrey Smithers, DSC, RN walked to the bows and looked over. Men were in the water and there was a deal of splashing. They were trying to get away from the coming suction as their ship went down.

He thought of Admiral Sir Christopher Cradock, and he shook his head. They didn't fight wars like that any more. He knew without false modesty that he was more useful to the Navy and his country alive and shooting at the enemy with all the experience he had garnered, than lying mouldering fathoms deep.

With a final look about him – he'd never forget *Melpomene*, never – he slid off the foredeck into the waiting water.

That sub – Hawkins, it was – he'd have to have a sharp word with him when they were picked up.

Infernal nerve!


The hunters came sniffing venomously after U-55.

Wolz dived deep.

The spine-chilling sounds of thrashing screws passed and re-passed. U-55 on her initial deep dive had taken a course to bring her out far to the south of the high-speed convoy.

Wolz wanted to load his last two spare torpedoes into the forward tubes and then surface to have another crack. He would lose the convoy if he was kept down; but he had to lie deep and doggo until the English lost him and gave up the hunt.

Then a high-speed dash on the surface might give him another chance before dawn. As the time ticked by he had to face the fact that he wouldn't be able to get ahead ready for another attack this night.

The jubilation in the boat was understandable and he felt he could allow the crew to expend a little of their feelings of success. He wanted every effort from them, and was determined to have it. But once the success was theirs, why, then, they could celebrate.

'A cruiser, skipper!' said Ehrenberger. He looked positively radiant.

'Only a light cruiser,' said Wolz. But he had to smile as he spoke.

Then the first depth charges dropped.

The shattering crashes thumped through the water. They smashed at U-55 and rolled her half-over. Crockery smashed in the galley. The lights went out and Lindner immediately started going round screwing in fresh bulbs, phlegmatically.

The next pattern was just that much further away to induce the crew of U-55 to imagine the Englishman was off on the wrong scent.

Wolz kept listening for that deadly pinging sound echoing against his steel hull. When it came he immediately altered course, speed and level. Three times he threw off the inhuman pinging, and three times the English picked him up again.

More depth charges sailed down.

U-55 was shaken like a rat in the teeth of a terrier.

As the lights smashed again and the valves cracked and a crewman leaped for a fractured pipe, Wolz corrected himself firmly. He had made up his mind before. He would not tolerate that image of a rat. Rather, he was the hunter temporarily being hunted.

Most of the crew had been through this nightmare before. That did not make the ordeal any easier to bear. The new hands had to be watched carefully, discreetly. The two Fahnrichs would now reveal more of themselves than had ever been revealed before.

Wolz took U-55 in a cunning underwater curve that traversed all three dimensions. He used the sea to cloak him in its immensity. But his submerged speed was around four knots, and the English destroyers, throttled down, could run rings around him.

The boat lurched as the next pattern exploded. The roar concussed gongingly against her plating.

'They don't give up,' remarked Ehrenberger.

'We'll lose them.' Wolz spoke confidently. 'Steer oh-oh-five. A hundred metres.'

U-55 nosed down.

The Mediterranean had many layers of water, layers that existed at different temperatures, and this fact was of great comfort to a U-boat commander.

If he could find one of these temperature gradients and cling stubbornly on, he could as it were hide. The probing beams of the asdic would reflect from the differing temperature layers and give readings that did not read true. Twice Wolz thought he had found a layer, and twice the cracking lash of the asdic returned to lay a whip of sound across his hull.

'Fifty metres. Steer two-seven-five.'

U-55 twisted and rose.

They all heard the massive detonations below them. The boat lifted, rearing, blown bodily upwards by the tremendous force of the explosions.

'Clear this rubbish away.' Wolz spoke in his cool contemptuous tones.

The litter of broken glass was swept out of the way.

Men chipped the jagged friezes of broken glass from the meter dials.

'Steer oh-nine-oh.'

U-55 turned, reaching blindly through the water.

He knew he had the depth under his keel. He could take her down until her pressure hull groaned.

The next pattern fell astern and still deep.

'Steady as you go. Quarter speed on port motor.'

Now the boat crept along, gently, seeking to sneak away.

The asdic vanished.

Then it returned with a monstrous ping that cracked against the steel hull and made them all jump.

The beat of screws over their heads seemed to force their heads down into their shoulders.

Wolz held on.

The asdic pings shivered against his steel hull, and faded. The low hum of dynamos sounded suddenly loud.

Wolz waited.

Presently, he was almost – almost! – satisfied that he had found a layer of colder water.

But in one very real sense he knew the English had beaten him.

He was steering oh-nine-oh, due east, and the convoy was drawing further and further away from him. The escorts had put him down and kept him down and driven him off.

They had failed to sink him.

But they had preserved their precious ships from him for this night, at least.


'Beg to report,' said Ehrenberger, and he tried unsuccessfully to kill his smile. 'Fähnrich Jagow dirtied his pants in the attack.'

'Really?'

Wolz felt the muscles at the sides of his mouth stretching, and he hauled himself back into imperturbable sternness.

U-55 drove on westwards on the surface, her diesels rumbling with health, and the sun shone and the sky shone a bright and beautiful blue, and life was very very good.

'Awful smell, skipper. Permission to rig a bucket and line?'

'Granted. They have to learn – and Thumen?'

'Didn't turn a hair. Mind you, skipper, it's early days yet. But I think in Fahnrich Thumen we have the makings of a U-boat officer.'

'Good. Well, carry on, Number One.'

'Very good!'

The situation might be humorous; but any added stink in a boat was a serious matter. All the expensive perfumes from Paris couldn't eradicate the typical U-boat aromas. Men had to live jammed in tightly together. But there was nothing he could say to the midshipman now; the damage had been done.

He did hear Leutnant Freyer, who did not get on with Jagow, mention the useful applications in future of a strategically placed cork.

Provided discipline was maintained and the men functioned as he wished, he was prepared to let them get on with their own relationships. He would step in with a most heavy hand if he suspected their antics could in any way jeopardise his command.

He could still hear, resounding and reverberating in his head, the creaking and cracking noises as the English cruiser sank. That long drawn groan of anguish as she slid beneath water chilled him in retrospect.

He had no wish to imagine the scenes that must have taken place.

A fine cruiser had been destroyed.

He, Baldur Wolz, had sent her to the bottom.

That was his job.

He shook the black mood off.

If a hostile aeroplane appeared and they had to dive suddenly, he did not want hands mucking about on the casing hauling in buckets of sea water to clean up that idiot Jagow.

He went up to the bridge and cast a cold eye down. Jagow looked thoroughly miserable. He looked cold and pinched, which in the bright Mediterranean sun made him appear even more woebegone.

No mercy for the youngster could be allowed to exist.

He was in a hard service, a harsh service, and he must learn.

Fear – that had to be used like anything else.

'Step lively,' Wolz called down.

The lookouts were fixed to their positions and scanning the sky with rapt attention.

God help them if they were not . . .

He felt itchy. There were far too many bodies swanning about on deck. Riepold had the watch.

Again he shouted down on to the casing where the bucket was just being drawn up, slopping and bouncing, spraying water.

'Make that the last! Jump!'

'Very good!' bellowed back Mueller, the elektro-maschinist. He seized the bucket and hoisted it in.

Just why Fahnrich Dietrich Jagow chose that moment of all moments Wolz would never understand.

The forward starboard lookout abruptly shouted, a high-pitched yell that brought everyone quiveringly alert.

'Aircraft! Green twenty!'

Wolz instinctively stared up, filled with rage. He ripped out the expected orders in a torrent of words.

The watch started to tumble below.

And Fahnrich Dietrich Jagow let out a shriek of pure terror.

He ran along the casing.

From the gun position he ran towards the bows, along the casing, without a slip or a stumble over the perforated steel. He screamed as he ran. His hair blew.

He ran like a maniac.

He leaped bodily off the boat and into the sea.

Mueller started after him. Mueller was a strong swimmer, and Wolz knew the seaman would grab the midshipman, give him a clip alongside the jaw, and swim back easily. But there was no time.

'Mueller! Halt! Get below! *Now!*'

Mueller swung back, opening his mouth, waving his arms.

U-55 was going down.

'Skipper –'

'Jump! You're on report!'

Sea water rose to break in angry foam across the forward casing. Loeffler in response to the dive command was putting U-55 below fast. Only Wolz remained on the bridge.

Mueller felt the angle of the boat under him. He twisted around. He saw the water, surging up in a white-spangled green breaking wall, roaring along the casing towards him.

U-55 slid deeper, going down fast.

The water foamed around Mueller. It swept him off his feet. His arms clawed the air and he went shooting back, sliding and losing his balance and so being swept away into the cataract of water. He fell over the side.

Wolz waited for no more.

Filled with that icy, terrible, mortifying rage, he ducked through the hatch. He slammed the lid with force.

Imbeciles! Idiots! Oafs!

U-55 plunged for the depths and Wolz dropped off the ladder in the control room.

He looked about him.

Everything looked normal.

'Thirty metres, Chief.'

Loeffler looked surprised. Everyone knew an aircraft was up there. At thirty metres down, U-55 was not as deep as they had come to expect their commander to dive.

Wolz said nothing.

'Thirty metres, skipper.'

'Catch a good trim. Prepare to surface in twenty minutes.'

'Very good.'

Pretty soon the buzz went around the boat that the idiot Fahnrich Jagow and old Mueller were missing.

The atmosphere thickened at once.

Ehrenberger looked studiously polite. 'D'you think they stand a chance?'

'They have one chance. They're in the Med.'

'Yes . . .'

Twenty minutes, Wolz was prepared to give that patrolling busy-body of an aeroplane. That could be cutting the margin too fine. But the itch he had felt had gone. Diving re-oriented a U-boat man, gave him new perspectives. Wolz did not think the plane would still be hanging around when he surfaced after twenty minutes or so.

Had he thought the RAF would still be aloft sniffing out for him, he would not have surfaced.

Two men's lives did not weigh against those of forty and the boat herself.

Not in Wolz's book.

The bearded faces of his men betrayed their different characters as they waited. Some men kept on glancing up so that the whites of their eyes gleamed like albumen. Others just stolidly concentrated on what they had to do. The big dials and the little dials; every one told a story, and Loeffler could read the story in a twinkling and know precisely what was happening in the boat.

The smell of Jagow hung in the air, and Freyer, who was more addicted to the scent bottle than the others, sprayed generously.

'Just refreshing the air for that wart Jagow,' he said to Thumen, with a lopsided smile.

'Yes.' The midshipman spoke slowly. 'I, too, think the skipper will bring him back safely, Herr Leutnant.'

'That's not quite what I had in mind.'

'Herr Leutnant Freyer!' said Wolz, suddenly, making all other conversations cease.

'Skipper!'

'Go and play your gramophone. Anything bar Wagner.'

'Very good!'

Freyer went off to the wardroom. Ehrenberger saw his commander's face, and he wondered – for the millionth time – just what gave Wolz this calm and ready air of knowing exactly what to do and the capacity of brain and muscle to do it. Freyer was a live-wire, no doubt of it. And Jagow was a wart. But . . .!

As for the commander of U-55 – he was feeling most thankful that he had come off well in two ways. If the plane up there had failed to spot the disturbance in the water as they dived – that was the first item to be thankful for. If the aircraft had spotted them then she could not have been of the type which carried depth charges or she had already expended them or they had hung up – that was the second item to be thankful for.

The English had undoubtedly made improvements in their depth charges. At the beginning the combatants had been faced with the farcical situation that one side's aircraft dropped bombs that were ineffective and the other side loosed torpedoes that did not work. But the farce was of a sour nature. For brave men risked their lives in planes and U-boats just to get into firing position, and they fired – and their weapons were useless.

Not much of a farce to the bloke in the middle, then . . .

The Herr Professor Dentz had talked about that on the afternoon following the shindig at the schloss. The penguin-man had not been seen all morning and Wolz guessed he was sleeping it off.

After lunch Dentz showed up.

'Let us not talk about last night, Herr Oberleutnant.' He sipped a Vichy water and he looked as though he had been run through a mangle. 'You were talking of the English wasserbomben – wabos, you fellows call them. I know. They didn't have anything they could drop from aircraft at the beginning. But they will make it hot for us in future.'

'They'll make it hot for me.'

'Quite so.' Dentz lifted a shaky hand. 'My head! But I insist on talking. I shall feel better – eventually.'

Wolz had to smile.

The Herr Professor's talk rambled. Wolz entertained the shrewd notion that the Vichy water was stirring up the alcohol remaining in the penguin-man's insides, and sending him off again. He started to talk of his association with Prince Borghese, and of what those fine fellows of the Tenth Flotilla MAS were up to. Wolz listened, fascinated by his complete lack of understanding of what the scientist was maundering on about.

'When they actually use their Maiale,' he said, shaking his head. 'By God; but it puts the shivers down your back.'

'I'm sure.'

'Hand me the bottle, will you, my dear fellow? I do feel peculiar.'

'I know very little about the Italian U-boats. Except in relation to their size and training methods.'

'Little ones, my dear Baldur – I may call you Baldur? – little ones. They're the secret.'

Suddenly the Herr Professor rocked forward in his chair. He pulled out an enormous coloured handkerchief, checked in yellow and brown, and began plastering it all over his face and mopping the sweat and blowing his nose. His eyes were running.

'Secret,' he said, blowing. 'Oh!'

'My dear Herr Professor,' said Wolz, earnestly. 'I have not heard or understood a word you've been saying.'

'I am glad. Please refrain from mentioning this – to anyone.'

Some spark fired up in Wolz then.

'I will. Except you. I am fascinated by what you are not telling me.'

The Vichy water went down in a gulp, Dentz made a grimace of distaste, and looked vaguely around as though expecting a magnum of champagne to appear magically at his elbow. In Uncle Siegfried's schloss when champagne appeared it was not miraculous but a normal part of ordered life.

'I can tell you nothing. Remember the SS-Standarten-führer last night? Well – be warned!'

'Of course. But – '

At that point Wolz was called to the telephone.

He went off fuming, wondering who the hell could be bothering him now, and determined to have a really serious onslaught on Dentz to find out more of these tantalising aspects of the U-boat war. After all, if anyone had a right to know what was going on, wasn't that a U-boat commander?

He picked up the phone.

'Baldur?'

He did not recognise the voice.

'Who is calling?'

'Is that Oberleutnant Baldur Wolz?'

'I might be able to find him if you tell me who is calling.'

'You are not Wolz?'

'Who is calling?'

The man's voice sharpened, became almost hysterical.

'Please fetch Oberleutnant Baldur Wolz immediately!'

'How do I know you're not an English spy?'

The remark was not entirely ridiculous, not entirely a joke. The man's voice held the trace of an accent Wolz did not place. A silence ensued. Wolz could hear the man breathing at the end of the line, and the distant and muted sound of a train. Then the sharp voice said: 'Tell Baldur Wolz that Karin wishes to talk to Wolfgang.'

Wolz closed his eyes. He held on to the phone as though it was a horseshoe-shaped U-boat lifebelt around his neck and the boat gone fathoms deep.

'All right.'

Trudi von Hartstein had called herself Karin when he'd driven her to the Bodensee. She'd called him Wolfgang. At the vivid sensory image of her that leaped into his brain he felt the leaping desire in him, unquenched, making him shudder with its violence.

'Well?' he said, and the menace in his voice sounded vicious.

'Wolfgang?'

'Yes, yes – get on with it, man!'

'You will meet Karin in the woods where you were riding a horse and a car burned. Two hours.'

The phone went dead.

# CHAPTER EIGHT

Trudi's appearance shocked him when they met under the shadow of the trees.

She looked thin. That was the only word for it. She was thin and gaunt, her cheekbones were pronounced, and her eyes held a feverish look. She continually licked her lips.

'Baldur! I knew you'd come —'

'What's it all about, Trudi. For God's sake!'

'I cannot tell you. I am all right — and you?'

'Yes, yes, the wabos haven't got me yet. But — you!'

'I do look a mess, don't I?'

She wore an old leather coat, cut short, and trousers, and a tiny felt cap pulled over her forehead. The trees shaded her face; but he could still see the heartbreaking loveliness of her, the glint of golden hair.

The face that was usually so pale and yet alive within that vibrant pallor was now just white, a dead white, and that scared Wolz. This girl was up to something and he didn't know what — wasn't sure if he wanted to know — and he had twice resolved to ask her to marry him.

'Did you bring it, Baldur?'

'Bring it? Bring what?'

'Oh, Baldur! You're not — not going to —' She was almost crying.

He took her arm. He shook that arm very gently.

'Bring what, Trudi? I don't know —'

'The money!'

'Money! Well, no one said anything about bringing money.'

She slumped. Her shoulders sagged.

'You see the sort of person I have to work with? I told – I told him to ask you to bring some money. All you could lay hands on at short notice. And he didn't?'

'Didn't say a word. If you want money,' and here Wolz made up his mind at once. Without a second thought. 'If you do, wait here. I can scrounge some, and Siegfried and Manfred are on leave and they'll – '

'No! You mustn't tell them . . .' Then, turning her head up to him, her eyes frantic, she said: 'Is Helmut in the schloss?'

'No.'

'Thank God!'

He was shaken. 'I won't tell my cousins what the money is for. We've always shared, as kids – even Lisl – well, that's all children's stuff, now. Can you wait here?'

'I must. I must have money – '

'You'll have it. I promise.'

'No questions?'

'Yes. But you won't answer them, will you?'

'I cannot.'

'You will not.'

'It is all the same.'

He kept his temper. Worn though she was, drawn and pale and limp, he wanted her. He faced that knowledge with a kind of horror from which he would not recoil. Cousin Lisl was denied him, as he believed, and the Lotties and Heidis and Marizas of this world were jolly romps. But this girl, this Trudi – yes, if he didn't love her then he was as close to that condition as a man could come.

'Have you seen Doctor Engel, Baldur?'

'Only that one time.'

'No matter. I think you would like to know that my mother is safe.'

Sharply, Wolz said: 'In Switzerland?'

'Yes.'

'I see.'

'No, Baldur, you do not see. But – the money – please. And take care.'

'I shan't be long –'

'I will wait.'

He went off, then, walking with his long strides, down from under the trees and out to cross the road and take the short cut. The Wolzes knew all the short cuts around here.

He fetched up with the road again a kilometre along and a shiny car drove around the bend. It was an Opel. It contained three men besides the chauffeur. They wore civilian clothes and Wolz sighed. If they were Gestapo – the car stopped.

Because it was now the custom, Wolz was wearing uniform. He saw the men looking at the dark blue cloth, the gold rings, the Iron Crosses. They wouldn't take him for a railway porter.

'Papers? Your papers, Herr Oberleutnant.'

There was no sense in arguing. He handed them across and when they came back after the briefest of scrutinies, the man with the scar along his jaw said: 'You have not seen anyone as you walked, Herr Oberleutnant?'

'No. I'm going back home and cut through the woods.'

'I see. If you see anyone acting suspiciously please contact the local –'

The other man, the one with the folds of neck hanging over his collar, let out an exclamation.

Over the brow of the opposite hill a man ran with a wild bounding pace. He ran down towards the road and then tried to angle back. Field glasses bounced on his chest. He wore civilian clothes.

Past him the figures of other men came into view, dark and ominous. They herded the chase down towards the road.

'That's him!' said pig-neck with immense satisfaction.

The fugitive abruptly stopped by a clump of bushes. Bright sparkles of flame broke from his hand. The sounds of the shots smacked flatly down to the road. One of the pursuers let rip with a burst of MP38 fire.

'The fool!' The man with the scar looked furious.

Up on the hill the man who had failed to ask Wolz to bring the money threw up his arms. He pitched into the bushes and was lost to view. Wolz surmised the man had been keeping him under observation and been flushed out. Trudi would have heard the gunfire. Now what would she do?

Wolz decided he had better look surprised and horrified. He started to shout out questions; but the scar-faced man – the scar was not a genuine duelling scar but a cosmetic artefact designed to impress – broke in impatiently.

'There are things which fighting men do not understand. Say nothing. An enemy of the Third Reich has met his death. And when I get my hands on the idiot who shot him I'll make him sorry.'

Pig-neck added: 'Now we'll never penetrate – '

But the car started and jerked away with a spurt of gravel and whatever it was that these gentry wouldn't now penetrate was lost.

All the time the third man, the one with the false beard and the monocle, had not spoken. Wolz fancied he would be the most dangerous of the three. These men were not play-acting. They were deadly serious about their business. And to cross them was to invite death. That had been the way to deal with Communists and Jews and homosexuals; it did not seem quite the same when it could happen to a serving officer of the Kriegsmarine.

The twenty minutes was up.

When Wolz gave the order to rise to periscope depth

his watch informed him that exactly nineteen and one half minutes had passed. He owed Mueller that half minute.

U-55 rose as the compressed air hissed. Loeffler was well aware of the critical problem here and he handled the boat beautifully.

'Up periscope.'

Wolz took a look around. A fast but thorough three sixty degree sweep of the sky first. Then the sea. Then down periscope.

'Very good. Take her up, Chief.'

Wolz stared around his control room.

'Stand by deck party. Heaving lines and lifebelts ready.'

'Very good!'

U-55 broke surface in a spouting of white water and Wolz was up through the hatch and staring all around, making absolutely sure not an enemy was in sight.

Only then could he start to look for Jagow and Mueller, assuming they were still alive.

It was Burmann, Mueller's oppo, who spotted the two dark figures. One was lifting in the water and waving an arm.

Wolz felt the pleasure run through him. He had contrived to run a course that had brought U-55 back to the spot where she'd dived. That pleased him.

'On deck, deck party. And make it lively!'

The hands raced on to the casing as U-55 eased down, turning to make a lee. The heaving lines and the lifebelts flew, arching through the air. Mueller got one lifebelt around Jagow, who looked like a lump of sodden seaweed.

They hauled the men aboard, fending them off the hard iron, and, dripping and laughing, Mueller waved buoyantly at the bridge. Wolz scowled down. He'd damn well take that grin off the elektro-maschinist's face!

These men of his were still keyed to operations in the

Atlantic. The heat of the Med had not yet got to them. But the usually cloudless skies and excellent visibility were not what U-boats wanted with English aeroplanes ready to leap on them at any moment. Wolz scowled some more as the bundle of old washing that was the still-breathing carcass of a Fahnrich of the Kriegsmarine was hauled inboard and humped down the tower. The men saw the scowl on Daddy's face and immediately they trod small.

Wolz was beginning to come to the conclusion that it just was not safe to steam on the surface in daylight in the Med. The wolf-pack tactics could not be put into operation because there were not enough German U-boats. The classical attack on the surface had been baulked when he'd tried for that convoy from which he'd plucked the cruiser. Well, he was after them on the surface and would have to go flat out to catch them now.

No more sighting reports had come in.

He wondered how many asterisks there were going up against the numbers of the U-boats in the lists at Kernevel. Donitz was dead set against disseminating his strength to the four corners of the world; but OKW had ordered this show of strength to the Med. If Gibraltar was to be rendered unusable to the English, if Malta was to be taken, if Rommel's supply lines were to be kept open, the U-boats just had to do the job.

The Italian Navy did not have sufficient fuel to sortie their big units in anywhere near enough strength. La Spezia and Pola would be the bases for the German U-boats, and Wolz harked back to what the Herr Professor Dentz had rambled on about the Italian U-boat men.

Life might prove interesting up there – 'Skipper?'

'Number One?'

'When do you want me to wheel Mueller in? Jagow is pretty far gone. He'll recover; but Otterndorf wants to keep an eye on him for a bit.'

'No time like the present, Kern. Wheel him in.'

'Very good!'

Now Wolz was faced with the kind of decision he would not normally have even been bothered with in the Atlantic.

If he ran along on the surface he knew he risked being spotted by a patrolling English aircraft. With this confounded perfect visibility allied to the translucency of the water he was going to be extraordinarily fortunate to get down safely every time. And he had the dark foreboding that the English aircraft were going to operate in greater and greater numbers.

But, if he dived so as to be safe whilst the court was in session, he'd lose time.

'Hold it, Kern. Belay that last order.'

'Skipper?'

'We have to keep going. That convoy is not going to hang around waiting for us to deal with that idiot Mueller.'

'Very good.'

So U-55 ploughed on across the blue blue Mediterranean, and the lookouts kept a most punctilious watch aloft.

Wolz fretted.

The day wore on and the watches changed and the men complained about the heat. It really was stifling in the pressure hull when the boat submerged. Wolz could allow no feelings of guilt that he stood on the bridge all the time. He might be in the bright fresh air; but on his shoulders rested the safety and the operational efficiency of his command.

Safety – now there was a difficult concept. He'd gone back to the woods with the money, and this time he'd been craftily careful, and avoiding the road had used the old byways and cuts they'd romped along as kids, pretending to be pirates and what not. Trudi had watched him approach from cover.

'You heard the gunfire?'

'Yes – ' Her gaze searched his face. She was breathing heavily. She had taken off the old leather coat to reveal a grey blouse that was a size too small for her and which did wonders for her figure and nothing at all for Wolz's morale. He wanted to take her in his arms – 'You have the money?'

'Here.' He handed across the thick roll of Reichsmarks. 'Siegfried and Manfred both coughed up. Told them I was a little short and I almost told them it was because a girl was in trouble.'

Now it was his turn to search her face as he made his feeble little joke.

'Thank you, Baldur. Now, perhaps – well, we will see.'

And then, she was in his arms, and he was kissing her lips, feeling their softness and moistness and warmth, and holding her body in the silly blouse, and hugging her to him.

'Trudi – '

'Baldur?'

He stepped back, shaking.

'No time now. I think – you were right to refuse when I tried to bribe you with – You helped me then. And again, now.'

'And you still will not tell me – ?'

She moved forward and put her arms about him. She moved gently. She kissed him. He felt the stars and the fireworks and he kissed her back with a passion she understood. She drew back. Her breathing was quick and light.

'Goodbye, Baldur – thank you – but – goodbye.'

She picked up her leather coat and, in an instant, was gone in among the trees.

He could have run after her – easily. He knew his way around these woods with their haunting childhood memories. He could have caught her – easily. He could have thrown her down, all warm and panting – easily. He could tear off that silly intoxicating blouse – easily, and pulled down her ridiculous trousers – easily. He could do all these things very easily – but he did not.

He stared helplessly at the trees, seeing the trunks tall and slender, and thick and gnarled, and the movement of the leaves, bright with summer warmth. He shook his head. What a fool he was!

She'd known about the death of her friend. Was that to be her fate as well? She had solemnly assured him that she was not doing anything to harm Germany or assist the country's enemies.

And now Wolz was in the Med and U-55 drove along the surface with her diesels rumbling throatily. He had to take into his consideration the growing problem of his nearness to Malta. He was quite prepared to go in under the guns, as it were; but that would have to be at night. He had to reconcile himself that his intended prey had given him the slip.

At the appointed hour the signal came in. At one stroke it rendered all his problems superfluous – rather, all the problems concerned with Malta and the convoy.

The signal presented him with a whole new batch of problems.

Holding the flimsy in his hands he became aware of Ehrenberger staring at him. The IWO would chew his fingernails over this one.

'Steer one-one-five.'

The quartermaster acknowledged. U-55 began to retrace her course. Ehrenberger's brows drew down. He pinched his lips.

'Crete?'

'No, Number One. The coast of North Africa,' Wolz told his second-in-command, half-smiling. 'Just east of Sidi Barrani. Egypt.'

# CHAPTER NINE

The German-Italian forces and the British Eighth Army had been locked fronting each other in a pseudo stalemate since the intensive battles of June. Tobruk continued as an irritation or a bastion, depending from which viewpoint it was seen. Rommel's supplies were being ravaged, as were those of the new Eighth Army commander. The battles of the desert consumed machines and material. It took ships to supply the insatiable needs of air forces, infantry and panzers alike. And the artillery never had enough shells.

Something big was brewing in the Eighth and because Rommel was not yet ready he played down the reports. Each side's supreme command kept urging attack, attack. And Eighth and DAK alike, when they attacked, burned up their tanks and panzers, and fired their ammunition, and cried out for more.

And, as well, men were killed . . .

U-55 slid through the sea towards her rendezvous.

Orders called for Wolz to pick up an officer off Derna. Then he would go on to the more mysterious rendezvous east of Sidi Barrani.

His calculations told him that he'd have just about enough fuel left, if he was not called upon for any high-speed dashes.

'Take us up, Chief,' Wolz called.

U-55 lifted as the compressed air hissed.

The depth indicators showed their ascent. Everything was in order. Loeffler had reported a minimal leak in the stern gland, port side, and Wolz would have to remember to use the starboard motor more than the port. U-55 lifted.

'Ten feet!' called Loeffler.

A few more moments, with Wolz and the bridge personnel waiting at the foot of the ladder.

'Tower clear!'

Wolz gripped the ladder and bundled up. As always as he unclipped and hefted the lid up the spray of water sluiced down on to his upturned face. He ought to remember to duck his head.

He slammed the lid back and climbed up to the upper hatch and then out on to the bridge. The time was right and the co-ordinates were right. He stared about, boxing the compass, ready to order a crash dive.

This close to the coast and the cover of the Luftwaffe the appearance of RAF aircraft would be more than unlikely unless he was supremely unlucky and had risen to the surface just as the RAF were indulging themselves in a bombing raid on the Afrika Korps.

The sky was clear, streaked with the oncoming evidences of night. But the light was still strong. He lifted his glasses and stared at the dun streak that was the coast of Africa to starboard.

The smell wafted out, strong and pungent, filled with spices, hot and exciting.

That was Africa over there . . .

'Switch control to bridge, obey telegraphs,' he said automatically. He kept on sweeping the horizon all around. The lookouts were up, almost knocking him over in their rush to their positions. There was a rush for them; that was as it should be. Loeffler knew the routine by now – switches off and shut down electric motors, clutches in.

'Half ahead starboard,' said Wolz. He had to nurse that port gland.

The bearings were taken as soon as the sextant was

brought up to the bridge, the land was a mere dun line; but the landmarks for which he looked as per the signal were there, and he was spot on. Any minute now.

'Aircraft green ninety!' sang out the starboard look-outs, almost together.

How odd not to bellow the instant order to flood and dive!

They watched the Fieseler Storch approach, wide winged, swinging over them in a graceful arc. There was no mistaking that silhouette.

'He can see us, that's for sure,' said Ehrenberger.

'Patience, Kern, patience. All will be revealed in due time.'

'When all my white hairs have fallen out.'

Still, you got used to secret missions when you were in U-boats.

The Storch circled again and then a dark bundle fell away from the slim fuselage. Moments later the 'chute opened. Wolz tasted the breeze, estimated the point of impact.

'Starboard ten.'

'Starboard ten.'

'Steady amidships.'

'Steady amidships.'

They watched the circle of the 'chute descending. Everything was very quiet and only the chugging of the diesel broke that stillness. The water moved with a long tired sigh.

'Stop engine.'

'Stop engine.'

Now U-55 ghosted forward. The water rippled along-side.

Wolz gave a few last minute finicky instructions to the helmsman and when the parachutist hit the sea they had him inboard within ten minutes. He came up on to the casing from his lifebelt shaking water from himself like an Airedale.

'Steer oh-nine-oh. Half ahead both. Kern – call me – you know. Send our visitor down to the wardroom, will you?'

'Very good!'

Ehrenberger would hand over the watch to Riepold as and when he chose. They were in for a haul and everyone wanted to get their head down and snatch as much sleep as possible.

In the wardroom Wolz turfed everyone out in the most polite way. He told Freyer to turn off his beastly record. There was no point in sitting in the captain's apology for a cabin. The wardroom seemed the place to receive his guest.

If that was unsociable, it would not be for long. Wolz just wanted to get this cloak and dagger stuff out of the way and go back to the important business of sinking ships.

'Leutnant Dieter von Rohwer, reporting aboard, Herr Oberleutnant.'

The tropical kit blazed in the wardroom. It seemed to bring all the colour and sunshine of Africa into the pressure hull. The Leutnant's sodden flying-gear had been stripped off and dumped somewhere by one of the hands. It would be safe in the boat. The tropical jacket and light-weight breeches had faded to a pale sandy colour. The high-laced boots looked well-worn. The ribbon of the Second Class and the medal of the First Class Iron Cross indicated that Leutnant von Rohwer was in the running for his Knight's Cross.

The Panzer Assault badge pinned below his Iron Cross at the bottom right hand corner of the jacket pocket indicated he had seen action in at least three panzer battles and gave meaning to the pink waffenfarbe. He smiled at Wolz, a big, burly man with crinkly brown hair and a high colour that had burned brown in sun and wind. He looked perfectly at ease.

'Oberleutnant Wolz, Herr Leutnant. Glad to have you aboard. And now, perhaps you will tell me what all this is about.'

'Brandenburg.'

Wolz nodded, keeping his face composed, waiting. He knew of the Brandenburg groups from what Siegfried had said, somewhat impatiently, about military intelligence setting up its own secret army. The Abwehr, run by Admiral Canaris, was a law unto itself, and that irked everyone else, who were laws unto themselves.

'You have heard of the Brandenburg organisation, perhaps?'

'Enough to know some commanders won't touch you with a barge pole.'

That high colour rose through the desert tan.

Von Rohwer nodded, a little too stiffly.

'That is so, I admit. But, also, I must say that it is the commanders who are blinkered in their outlook. War is war and modern war is modern war – we were in Poland before the first panzers crossed the border.'

'I'm more interested in what you wish for at the moment. I am not too plentifully provided with fuel, and I have only two eels in my forward tubes – '

'Torpedoes will not be necessary, Herr Oberleutnant. At least, I devoutly hope so.' He saw Wolz's face, and went on quickly. 'I have the exact co-ordinates. We are to rendezvous and pick up a Brandenburg group from the beach.'

'You want me to run in close, then? The airboat won't take an army.'

'There should be a dozen. If they have taken casualties, well . . .' Von Rohwer lifted his left hand an inch from the wardroom table and then let it drop.

Wolz saw something of what had been going on behind British lines in that movement. Very nasty.

He'd have a dozen men extra jammed into the cramped pressure hull. A dozen soldiers, with clumping great boots and being seasick everywhere and getting in the way. He sighed.

The panzer officer saw that reaction.

'In the Brandenburg we can turn our hands to many things. At the moment I masquerade with pink waffenfarbe. You will find the group you pick up will not inconvenience you.' He looked carefully at Wolz, as though summing him up. Finally, he said : 'I think it best you should know that an Italian U-boat was designated for this duty. She failed to report her position and is presumed lost.'

'I see.'

Well, that did explain it . . .

Also, it brought up unpleasant ideas. If the Italian U-boat had been sunk, it could mean the English were aware of what was going on and would be ready for him . . . Even nastier . . .

'Perhaps now, Herr Oberleutnant, you will assign me to my quarters?'

Wolz moved his hand in a nonchalant circling gesture.

'You are sitting in them, Herr Leutnant. You will have to take whatever bunk happens to be empty from watch to watch.' He saw with pleasure the lack of reaction in the Brandenburg opposite. 'We are like sardines in U-boats.'

'That will be perfectly correct. They took my equipment away — '

'Equipment?'

'Radio, signalling lamp, one or two odds and ends.'

'They'll be safe. The Cox'n will know. Now, if you will excuse me, Herr Leutnant, I must go to the bridge.'

Von Rohwer put his right hand on his tropical field cap. It was bleached almost white. Around his right sleeve the cuff title AFRIKAKORPS in silver embroidery on dark green caught the light. It hardly glittered at all.

'Very good!'

If the Brandenburg's wearing of the cuff title was genuine and not a part of the cloak and dagger nature of his unit, it meant he had served in Africa for at least two months. The cuff title had been authorised only on 28th July.

Faded sleeve and cuff title, brown hand, bleached tropical field cap, they summed up this fellow. He took his cap off the table and stood up as Wolz rose.

'Carry on, Herr Leutnant,' said Baldur Wolz.

That, he felt as he went through the control room and up the ladder, was sufficiently navy to make the point with the Brandenburg.

The thick growths of beard decorating the U-boat men's grimy faces and the reek of the boat herself had not seemed to discommode Leutnant von Rohwer one wit. He must have a strong stomach. Just let him wait until they'd been kept down for twelve hours – then they'd see how strong his guts were!

And twelve hours was not by any means a limiting factor when you had your head down and the English destroyers were tumbling their awful wabos on top of you . . .

Commanding a U-boat was a matter of knowing what to do and when to do it, and knowing right away you had made the right decision. More often than not – thank God not always – if you made the wrong decision you and your crew were dead.

All the usual routines had to be routine, and, always in a U-boat, they had to be handled with extraordinary attention all the time. Flooding to dive, blowing to rise, grouping in, switches out, lookouts up and down, hatches shut or opened, depth gauges, inclinometer, all the myriad of dials and levers – all existed as separate things in their own right and all had to be made to exist in a framework of inter-dependence that added to the skill and devotion of the men handling the boat made life reasonably secure and success a strong probability.

As a U-boat commander you just did not think of the routine and you thought of nothing else. Doing the right action at the right time had to be automatic. And, as well, you had to know you were doing it right all the time.

No wonder the lines of Wolz's face grew more graven with every patrol. But, on this cruise, he could report a great success. He had sunk an English cruiser. No doubt BdU would discover her name in time, and signal the news to the commander of U-55.

The cruiser was a species of feather in his cap. His main object was to sink freighters, for they carried the sinews of war. But it was nice to have a cruiser under your belt. He could not add her displacement to the total of gross tonnage he claimed; but she would go in the same score box as the AMC and any other warship Wolz sent to the bottom.

U-55 maintained a steady twelve knots, her MAN diesels thunking out with throaty power. The leak from the port gland worried Wolz a little, for he knew that Loeffler would have it under constant scrutiny. All the same, when Ehrenberger came on the bridge Wolz took himself off aft to have a look for himself.

As he went aft accompanied by Loeffler he heard Steidle, who acted as his steward, mumbling to himself about the state of the skipper's clothes when he wrapped himself around the shaft. Wolz ignored Steidle. He was a hunched-up little man, wiry, who came from Augsburg and could make the best coffee out of ingredients that were not any brand of coffee that Wolz knew.

'Looks unhealthy, Chief. What's your verdict?'

Loeffler screwed his fierce red beard around. It seemed to spit flame in the erratic light of the handlamp. The confined space compressed grotesque shadows about them. Like most places in a U-boat, the bulkheads and hull ran with condensation.

'It'll last us to La Spezia, skipper. But I'd not run up too long – there's a nasty kink somewhere. The depth bombs did us a power of no good back there.'

'Yes. Well, I'll try not to run too fast if we're chased.'

Watching the skipper wriggling back along the tunnel, Loeffler felt a remarkable desire to laugh. Baldur Wolz could put his finger on the itch, that was undeniable.

Back on the bridge in the fresh air he saw the blur of sand-coloured uniform, standing over by the port lookout forrard.

'Herr Leutnant von Rohwer? Kindly go below decks at once.'

'Herr Oberleutnant?'

Wolz kept it punctilious.

'You will obey my orders, if you please. Go below!'

The Leutnant understood the bite of command in that voice. But his sunburned face looked angry. He went to the hatch and lowered himself down.

Wolz, in order to hammer home the point, leaned down and bellowed so that all could hear in the control room.

'Cox'n! I will not have my orders disobeyed. No one comes on the bridge without my permission.'

'Very good!' bellowed Lindner in reply.

Wolz just hoped that Hans Lindner understood the reason for that superfluous, and insulting, command. The cox'n was a man highly valued by Wolz – he valued all his men who knew their jobs and were steady and reliable and had that extra flair he so much prized – and he supposed a mere petty officer would have some difficulty in stopping an officer. But, all the same, the idea of having gawking passengers lollygagging on his bridge sent the cold shivers down his spine.

He knew a little of the Brandenburg operations. Siegfried had not seemed too pleased. And Wolz would give a dozen of these Brandenburg fellows for one Hans Lindner, cox'n of his U-boat.

There was no gainsaying the quiet cold presence of von Rohwer. It remained to see if that was merely all uniform and decorations and façade.

Steering east into seas which were flanked by a hostile land controlled by the English, Wolz edged out into the offing. He dropped the coastline to starboard. He had the charts out and, not without irony, many of them were British Admiralty issues, impeccable examples of the navigatory and cartographic expertise of the nation with whom he was at war.

He left the bridge to the watch. There was no need to threaten dire retribution for any dereliction of duty. They all knew, the WO and the lookouts, that a very nasty death could result if they failed in their duties.

The blue lamp threw strange shadows across the control room where the red night lights glowed eerily. Men's faces appeared starkly from the red-tinted shadows.

'Here,' said von Rohwer, stabbing his finger down.

He had made no comment on Wolz's brusque order. No doubt someone had told him of the regulations governing just who was on the bridge at any given moment.

Wolz studied the soundings.

'Not too bright.' He allowed his mind to form a kind of three-dimensional picture the lines showed him. 'Like the Med. All up and down.'

'The men will be off very smartly once they receive the signal.'

'With half the Eighth Army breathing down their necks?'

Von Rohwer straightened. He was a big fellow, right enough.

'I trust it will not come to that.'

'I trust, also. But I refuse to hazard the safety of my boat.'

'My orders are —'

'I'll take you in, von Rohwer. You'll give your signal and you'll receive the correct acknowledgement before I lower the airboat over the side. And I must warn you — if there is the slightest sign of trouble, I shall pull out.'

'I understand, Herr Oberleutnant. Very good!'

# CHAPTER TEN

Wolz sat at the wardroom table, flanked by Ehrenberger and Freyer – Riepold had the watch – and stared grimly at Elektro-Maschinist Mueller. Wolz contained the annoyance that his officers, who had been on watch and would go on watch, could not get their heads down but had to sit in judgement on an idiot.

'This is a ship's court martial, Mueller. You understand?'

'Yes, Herr Kapitän.'

The formality of that suited the occasion. Mueller's grimy bearded face shone with sweat. He stood stiffly, hands at his sides, at attention. He looked pretty green.

'I wonder if you do, Mueller. It means if you are found guilty you can be shot and thrown over the side.'

Mueller swallowed. The whites of his eyes gleamed.

'You heard my order – it was unnecessary when the order to dive had been given. But you chose to ignore it.'

'I thought –'

'Yes?'

'The Fahnrich – he had to be brought back –'

'You've served with me before, Mueller. You are a U-boat man. Yet you forgot the most elementary of lessons.'

'Yes, Herr Kapitän.'

'Have you anything else to say in extenuation?'

'The boat dived very rapidly, Herr Kapitän. The sea caught me unprepared.' Mueller looked a little rebellious.

'But for that I'd have been all right. I was on my way back.'

'You are saying you were in the act of obeying my order – a lawful order from a superior officer – when the sea swept you over the side?'

'Yes, Herr Kapitän.'

Thank God Mueller had had the sense to be led.

'I see.' Wolz's stony face was putting the fear of the devil up Mueller. 'I shall reserve my decision as to the nature and extent of your punishment. But I accept your story. The boat did go down rapidly. I think you will have pay stoppages and privileges revoked.' He looked up with great meaning at Mueller. 'I do not think this kind of nonsense will happen again. Not to you or any other of the crew. But, if it does, just remember – next time I shall not put back for you. Is that clear?'

'Yes, Herr Kapitän.'

'Very good. Carry on.'

When Mueller had stumbled aft out of the wardroom back to the stern ends where, no doubt, he would be set on by his engineer comrades to tell them all about what Daddy had said, Wolz relaxed.

Hans Lindner who had stood silently all the time at Mueller's elbow nodded briskly.

'Carry on, Cox'n.'

'Very good.'

Fahnrich Thuman, at the end of the table, looked up from his notes. His pen poised. Wolz said: 'Now we come to the problem of Fahnrich Dietrich Jagow. I remand him for medical attention. Let it so be entered in the record.' He looked around. 'The Court is now dissolved.'

Then, before anyone else could speak, he added sharply: 'And go and get your heads down. We have a big night ahead of us.'

'Very good!' they chorussed. Wolz yawned, rubbed a

hand across his forehead, and then went over to take the papers from Thumen. The midshipman looked up with an apprehensive glance.

'Will – will they be very rough on Dietrich, skipper?'

'That lies with the doctors. He'll be turned out of the U-boat arm, I feel sure. Maybe he will be drafted to the Russian Front. Maybe he will be lucky and go to a big ship. Well,' and here Wolz yawned again. 'Maybe that won't be so lucky, at that.'

'No, skipper.'

Wolz went into his tiny cabin and pulled the green curtain across. He lay on his bunk and shut his eyes and could not rest. Riepold was perfectly capable, a fine officer. U-55 was in good hands. Wolz just had to learn the knack of ceasing to worry all the time he was not on the bridge, when the boat was surfaced, or in the control room when she ran deep.

He tried to think of Mariza, the time they'd fallen into the bath filled with suds together, and made love there, all hot and steamy and squishy, and his tired brain kept bringing up vivid sensory pictures of Trudi.

By God! She'd looked terrible. The dark smudges under her eyes, that drawn wan look of exhaustion on her face, and that silly infuriating grey blouse that outlined her figure in voluptuous detail. He wanted to take her in his arms and put her head on his shoulder and comfort her, just holding her, just feeling their bodies touching, close, companionable.

What the hell was the girl up to?

And Helmut – she was clearly in mortal terror of Cousin Helmut. Well, Helmut was Gestapo. Many people must go in mortal fear of Cousin Helmut, and yet he remained always on good friendly terms with his cousin, Baldur Wolz, and they could still laugh and talk of the old days as children. Was this what war did to other men, men who did not dive beneath the sea and sink helpless ships and topple their crews into a blazing sea?

The speaker in the overhead squawked into his ear.
'Kapitän to the bridge!'

Wolz was off the bunk and out past the green curtain and flying through the control room and up the ladders. He burst on to the bridge, shoving his night-vision glasses up out of the way and following the pointing line of Riepold's arm.

He blinked.

It took longer than he liked to see the smudges to starboard.

'Four of 'em, Skipper. Not large. Coasters –'

'Trying to slip into Tobruk. Not big enough for an eel . . .'

Leutnant von Rohwer shouted up from the tower.
'Permission to come on the bridge!'

That made sense and Wolz barked down confirmation. When the Brandenburg joined them he started to speak at once.

'Herr Oberleutnant! Your duty is to pick up my men – there is no time for anything else. And you will betray –'

'I know.'

Riepold coughed.

The 8.8 cm would finish off the coasters well enough. The English were even using sailing ships to smuggle supplies into besieged Tobruk. And for every ton of cargo sunk that number of Afrika Korps men's lives could be saved.

'Herr Oberleutnant – my orders –'

'Please keep silent, Herr Leutnant.' Wolz spoke mildly. 'I will make the decision.'

Von Rohwer turned away so sharply he collided with the periscope standard, and cursed, and lurched to stand looking over to starboard at that little squadron of four blockade runners. His fists clenched.

The breeze whispered from the north-west, a mere zephyr, and the stars glittered, fat and bright and very close. In the darkness they covered the whole sky, blazing. When a man stood isolated and looked up at the stars the immensity of the presence reached down and shrivelled his soul. A man could grow very frightened just by looking up at the stars. Who knew What was Out There . . .?

Wolz made up his mind.

'Gun action. Stand by gun's crew. Break open the ammunition locker.'

'Herr Oberleutnant!' The Brandenburg's voice rose. He was livid with anger.

'Silence in the boat! We don't want the Tommies to hear us before we send 'em over our little presents.'

Von Rohwer subsided. But it was perfectly clear Wolz had not heard the last of this. There would be repercussions. All he knew was that he had time before the rendezvous the following night and his job was to sink ships that were helping Rommel's enemies.

The new 2-cm flak gun they had picked up at Naples could now be tested out in fine style.

The guns were manned and ready. Without appearing to take his eyes off the four targets sailing steadily on, Wolz made sure that he saw the screwed tampion removed from the muzzle of the 8.8. He did not want a splayed gun barrel and bits of dead men scattered over his casing.

He studied the four dark shapes. Not above a few hundred tons each, they coasted along in line astern. He gathered that it was quite likely they were manned by detachments from the British Army rather than the Royal Navy. That would help. Should he handle them like a cavalry charge or like a duck-hunter? If he hit the lead ship first the others might run on to port of her and so seek to escape observation in the flame and smoke. If he picked the last one first, the leaders might turn instantly for the shore. Pick the last. That way the others would have to sail on without the protection of smoke cover.

'Aim at the stern vessel.' He spoke quietly but briskly. 'The Flak aim for the second ahead. And don't miss. I'll give you orders when to switch aim.'

'Very good.'

The gunners had donned their steel helmets, as regulations demanded, and they looked odd in a U-boat. The long barrel of the 8.8 swung to lower down on the English ships. Of course, they could not spot the pencil slim shape of his boat in the sea.

Visibility was excellent with that gorgeous gathering of stars and the edging appearance of the moon, and the English would probably see him when he opened fire. He wondered what they had in the way of armament. A few Brens, perhaps a Bofors. Yes . . . He leant down at the rear of the conning tower and spoke quietly to the 2-cm crew.

'The moment they open fire shift your aim to their guns. Knock them out. And be brisk about it.'

'Very good.'

He had a good crew. Officers and men knew their jobs.

He looked across at the ghosting shadows of the boats out there, and he sighed at this wanton destruction and said: 'Fire!'

The cracking smack of the 8.8 ripped the silence of the night to shreds.

The lurid dart of flame blinded everyone.

But the gunners had the range and as the breech clanged open and the next round was thrust in, Wolz, clapping his night-glasses to his eyes, stared eagerly at the target.

As often happened the first shot was a beauty.

The flash of flame spurted up from that dark silhouette.

The 2-cm was pumping out its little shells, and as Wolz switched his viewpoint he knew that although he couldn't see what was going on there, the Flak was hitting home.

The 8.8 belched again.

The gun crew worked like demons, the long brass cartridge cases clattering and sliding on to the casing.

A bright wink of light opened up on the third ship astern.

That was a Bren. The Tommies had reacted quickly, then. In the next moment the Bren ceased fire. The U-boat's flak had drawn blood . . .

A Bofors began to hammer out patterns of five shots from the lead ship. Instantly the 2-cm switched fire. For an incredible moment the tracers criss-crossed like rapiers. Then the Bofors, too, fell silent. The stern ship was burning fiercely, hurling long streaks of orange fire across the dark waters.

Other guns opened up. The 2-cm flak hammered away. The 8.8 switched to the next ship on Wolz's command, and then he saw the burst of fire from the dead centre and snapped out the order to shift to the second in the line.

The lead ship was turning. He could see the dark smudge of shadow drawing in and narrowing. He wanted to yell and bellow his men on; but they were shooting superbly.

A crewman at the 8.8 abruptly let out a shrill, shocked yell. He staggered. He was carrying the long gleaming brass and steel 8.8 cm round in his arms. He lurched. His steel helmet fell off. He staggered to the side, tried to recover. Wolz saw the dark stain across his sweater, all across his back.

He fell down, and rolled over, still clutching the long slender cartridge case.

It was Ludwig Hirsch.

Only the leaping flash of a light-coloured jacket and the sudden galvanic effort at the breech of the gun told Wolz that Leutnant von Rohwer had joined the struggle. The Brandenburg would know how to handle an 8.8 cm . . .

Little high-pitched pinging sounds sparked up from the steel hull . . . They were machine gun bullets. Wolz searched the enemy ships for the tell-tale wink of flame. He spotted it spurting from the least damaged vessel and bellowed his flak gun on to the target. Moments later the Bren that had killed Ludwig Hirsch fell silent.

'Get that lead ship!' shouted Wolz.

The other three vessels were now burning with a ruddy glow casting a lurid light upon the water. Beyond them the stars were obscured by the masses of smoke.

The 8.8 swung around, the long barrel snouting.

The ship was fast vanishing, stern on, dwindling away into the darkness.

They had just four shots, and Wolz was prepared to swear that each shot struck. But nothing happened. For a long moment Wolz stared into the shadows past the burning wrecks, and he wanted to curse deep in his throat.

'Three,' he said.

The night turned into day. The light blossomed in the sky and spread and stained the water with blood. The world was illuminated. The sound followed, a solid wall of noise, slapping their heads back as though they had run full into a heavyweight punch from Max Schmeling. Their ears rang. The sea jumped. U-55 leaped like a salmon.

When he could see and hear again, Wolz shouted out: 'Ammunition ship! Well done! Secure from gun action. Bridge watch on deck only. Steer oh-seven-five. Full ahead both!'

The activity repeated itself, this time in reverse, as the tampion was screwed in and the gun secured. The crews tumbled down. U-55 swung around towards the north-east and white water kicked back from her stern.

Like the steel shark she was, the U-boat raced away from the scene of her victory and the inevitable retribution that would follow and which would – if they were unlucky – sink her.

# CHAPTER ELEVEN

Oblt . z. S. Baldur Wolz felt that despite the difficulties flung in his path by all manner of unexpected happenings, he was at last beginning to set about the task he had been sent into the Mediterranean to perform.

Mind you, four miserable little coasters, dhows or rubbish skips, most of them, probably, were not much to show. But the garrison in Tobruk would have that much less grub to eat, that many gallons of petrol less to fuel their armour, that quantity of shells and bullets less to shoot at the Afrika Korps.

And, he could always conjure up the warm feeling created by the cruiser.

Like a lethal steel shark, thrumming with power and purpose, U-55 slid along at fifty metres. Topsides the sun was shining and the English flyboys would be angrily seeking prey.

Inside the cramped and stuffy confines of U-55 life rolled along. Watches changed, Smutje served up the food – some of it was still quite palatable – and the coffee was still holding out. The hydrophone operator, Willy Marwitz, was off duty, and Heinrich Stoller sat in the radio compartment with his hands clamped over the earpieces. All around them the mystifying and infuriating Mediterranean stretched, breathing with noise, through which Stoller must search for the first ominous beat of propellers. The control room was in the capable hands of Riepold and Lindner, and Loeffler was away aft again puttering over his diesels. They had been sparking lately, and two of the diesel room machinists had been burned.

Loeffler did not care for that kind of thing.

Wolz kept to his tiny cabin, disinclined for conversation. As far as he could see there was nothing left to say about the coming night's escapade. The quicker it was over the better. Then he'd hightail it for base and pick up fresh supplies and a new outfit of eels and be off to see what he could do about drawing the stranglehold on Malta closer, or perhaps coming back for another crafty crack at the blockade runners into Tobruk, or even ranging further afield in search of the ships creating havoc with Rommel's seaborne supply lines.

All in all, he needed these few precious hours of rest and recuperation.

The stuffiness of the boat was not too unpleasant, although he realised that von Rohwer must be suffering. To a U-boat man the stink although noxious became a mere part of routine. Someone from the fresh air being suddenly placed inside the pressure hull would have turned green and brought up his lot.

The deep rumble of von Rohwer's voice reached Wolz as he half-drifted off to sleep, talking about the Brandenburg leader in Africa, von Koenen, and graphically describing the blowing up of English fuel and ammunition dumps. That was what these dozen men he was due to pick up had been about, he surmised. Well, no doubt they'd turn green and puke the moment they descended into the dolorous insides of U-55.

Poor old Freyer had turned green and puked that night he and Ehrenberger and Riepold had persuaded their skipper to visit a maison in Paris. Wolz didn't care for the places much; but the French girls appeared to have been picked with care and they looked clean and bright. To the victor the spoils. These girls were trying to earn a living, and this was the thing they were best at. But the place got on Wolz's nerves. Plush, tawdry glitter, with expanses of half-naked female flesh, garters and black stockings and ribboned bows. He made a quick excuse and took himself off. Poor old Freyer – poor young Freyer. He'd do better to stick around his Wagner records.

At the time he'd been waiting for U-55 to finish her lengthy repairs. Loeffler stayed with the boat. The officers went up to the Baltic in between periods of leave. Wolz had had enough of the Baltic in one sense, but he realised that if he could help lick new U-boat men into shape then he was making a valuable contribution to the war.

There was no suggestion that he should get another boat. There were few enough of them, anyway.

When he had managed to wangle some fresh leave and re-visit his uncle's schloss he found the place looking just the same, bowered in greenery, solid and comfortable, filled with the warmth of sunshine and home and the richness of the countryside. The journey here had been exhausting. He could look at the schloss and feel the serenity reaching out to welcome him home.

Liszt's fanfares were used before important announcements of victories. More than one convoy battle report had been ecstatically broadcast over the air to the German people. Now, as Wolz walked quietly up to the main gate with the stone eagles and griffins, he reflected that the latest announcement left a great deal to be pondered on. He had to admit, a sailor though he might be and no soldier, the idea gave him goose pimples.

War with Russia !

And England still not fully knocked out.

It made a fellow think.

His uncle met him with his usual kindness. He was quite clearly preoccupied. Now this fresh war had begun Uncle Siegfried was going to be fully engaged in massproducing the artefacts of war. Wolz was aware that his uncle worked as he did in order to place first-class weapons in the hands of the troops, and not for the profit thereby entailed.

'I don't know what to think, my boy. I just do not know.'

'We beat them before – Tannenberg – '

'Yes, yes, I know, and Samsonov killed himself. But they were a different people then.'

'Not Communists, you mean?'

'Precisely. I, we have to fight them, there is no doubt of that. They pretended friendship so as to stab us in the back the moment they were strong enough. At least the Führer has stopped that little plot.'

'Siegfried and Manfred? They're in it I suppose?'

'I expect so. They wouldn't have told me, of course.'

'They'll be all right. Why, the Wolzes are always all right.'

'It is Helmut who worries me, Baldur. I remember him as a child, a laughing youngster, full of fire and spirit. But now – I wonder just what has been going on in Germany.'

'What has been going on, uncle, as you very well know, is that we have regained our self-respect. We are once more a great nation in the world. That means a great deal.'

'Yes.' Uncle Siegfried looked up as his secretary Mariza walked with her lithe step into the room. 'Well, I just make weapons. What they do with them – I suppose that is their business.'

Wolz was looking at Mariza. He saw the quick flash of an expression he could not define cross her features; then she was composed, and smiling, and greeting him.

'Baldur!'

'Mariza – '

'Champagne,' broke in Uncle Siegfried. He rubbed his hands together as though to rid himself of unwelcome thoughts. 'I've had a few dozen crates delivered in. Fine French vintage; but then, Baldur you devil, I don't have to tell you about vintages, do I?'

'You may tell me as much as you like, uncle, and I shall listen – and sample them, too!'

Mariza laughed.

When the champagne came in Wolz tasted and smiled, and supped. This, at the least, was something in the world.

The look Mariza gave him over the rim of her glass added to his feeling of sudden wellbeing. Everything was going to turn out all right. There was champagne and a girl and a comfortable home – and, really and truly, when you came to think about it, it wasn't what you could *really* call war on two fronts, was it?

One particular nightmare that could unfailingly unnerve Baldur Wolz tortured him that night.

The interior of the U-boat glimmered all about him, festooned with condensation, dim in the blue emergency lighting, with the shriek of escaping compressed air whistling like demented creatures of darkness in his ears. The pressure hull shook with the detonations of the depth charges. They were so near that in the instant before each exploded the sound of the hydrostatic valves opening with their twin clacks, a macabre indication of enemy technology at work deep beneath the sea, prepared his cringing body for the thunderclap.

The boat was not U-55 – it never was U-55.

The pressure hull was smashed in as though Odin's hammer had crunched down full on the tough Krupp plating.

Water boiled and roared and gushed into the boat.

Black, solid, impenetrable, the water was rushing into the compartment where he stood gripping to an invisible bar of iron, holding on for dear life. He was within two strides of the watertight door and its round heavy hatch.

And the nightmare was this – his duty called on him to close the door immediately so that the water should not rush entirely through the boat and drag her to the bottom. He must shut the door at once, and he was on the wrong side. When he shut the watertight door and stopped the onrush of the water he would be trapped. The compartment would fill and he would drown.

He had to shut the door off, stop the onrush of water, and he had to kill himself in doing his duty.

The nightmare tormented him that he would not have the courage to do this terrible thing.

He sweated and thrashed and reared up with a shriek, the bedclothes tangled about him, wet with sweat, safely in his own bed in his own room in the schloss. He glared wildly about. He had been there – *in* the boat – and she was going down, and the water pouring in . . .

He swallowed down. He was shaking and trembling and his body was wet all over.

The door opened and a candle poked through. A white form followed. For an instant he thought he was still dreaming and he'd been sucked down in the sinking boat and now here were the ghosts of the undersea come to chew the flesh from his bones.

'Baldur? Baldur – are you all right?'

'Yes. Yes. Perfectly, thank you.'

She came into the room and closed the door at her back. Her hair was down. She held the candlestick up and the radiance in falling across Wolz in the bed half-fell across her body, also, highlighting and shadowing her shape in the white nightdress.

'You were making an awful row.'

'Bad dream.'

'U-boats?'

He hesitated. But there was no use pretending.

'Yes.'

She did not smile. She approached the bed and put the

candlestick on the side table beside his watch and wallet and money. Then, with a sweeping movement of the skirts of the nightdress, she swept them aside and sat down on the bed facing him.

'I suppose it was that awful chlorine gas.'

'No –'

'Can you tell me? It might help.'

'I don't think so.'

'You look terrible.'

'And you look – lovely.'

Mariza Kalman, his uncle's secretary, did indeed look lovely in these surroundings. Normally she wore sensible clothes and flat-heeled shoes, with a pair of gold-rimmed glasses perched on her nose and her mousey hair firmly done up in a bun at the nape of her neck. But when she played the games with her friends, when she looked as she appeared now, she was transformed.

She was from Vienna, and Wolz suspected there was Hungarian blood in her, to give her that dark, full, somehow secretly seductive look. Yet she was a prim miss during office hours.

'I think,' she said, and her words although perfectly audible, were soft and breathless, 'I really think, Baldur, that you must take another bath. You are all sweaty. I shall scrub your back for you –'

'As you did last time?'

She looked down at the tumbled bedclothes. A pink tongue-tip crept out. Then she looked directly at him. 'As I did last time.'

So once again the bathroom with its mirrors and gold-plated taps filled with scented steam. The foam frothed splendidly. Wolz was very severe and would not allow the water level to rise past Mariza's nipples, for, as he said: 'You can always flood and dive if you wish.' To which she replied with a shake of her brown hair: 'And if I blow and rise?'

There was only one answer to that.

His casual talk of U-boats rubbed off on her. That bath night was the first one on this leave of many. During the day when she was not engaged with his uncle they would walk in the grounds and sometimes take a picnic into the woods, where it always ended in the same way. Once she said to him that wasn't it disappointing, wasn't it a shame, that he trained up a crew and then had half of it taken away when he went on the next cruise, to take a bunch of greenhorns and train them up?

'Not really. And the training flotillas are pretty strict. They chuck out the duffers. And I know that most of my own crew will be with me when I – '

'When?'

'If I knew that I'd be less jumpy.'

He had a letter from Willi Weidmann who wrote in his usual bumbling way about his successes and failures, all in guarded language. His dugout canoe was being fully occupied. And, also, there was a letter from Rudi von Falkensbach. The 'von' was, as always with Rudi, shortened to a mere 'v' and this, Wolz had to admit with a smile, was real style.

Rudi and his boat – he could not quote the number but Wolz knew – were due to finish up in the Baltic. Wolz hoped he might see something of his old comrade when he rejoined the flotilla; but that was not to be.

There was no letter from Cousin Lisl, and this depressed him. He had perforce put her out of his thoughts. Whilst he toyed with the Marizas of this world, as he so often told himself, he felt bound up with Trudi von Hartstein. The similarity in the names of Rudi and Trudi had never escaped him. He had more than once considered it an omen.

But as an omen of what he hadn't the faintest idea . . .

Uncle Siegfried could tell him little of Lisl.

'She was always a girl of enormously strong will, you know, Baldur. I remember once she had you four boys in terror of your manhood for a whole week – you must all have been ten or twelve at the time – and what the original argument was about I have no idea.'

'I believe I have forgotten, too, uncle.'

It was less of a strain on boyish terrors to forget. Lisl had waved the carving knife and they'd believed her – by God, they'd believed her! They'd taken it in turns to keep watch in Siegfried's bedroom. Three of them had slept by turn and one had stayed awake. Siegfried was the eldest. They'd spent five nights like that. Then Lisl had put the carving knife back in cook's kitchen drawer and they'd all gone off to a camp in the woods where they'd cooked sausages over a smokey wood fire. Old days, bright and dark – but Lisl knew her own mind.

She was removed from Wolz himself, he knew, a star that he could never pluck from the sky.

'She joined one of these organisations that proliferate and wear amazing uniforms and do – well, what, I do not know.'

'So long as she is safe and happy.'

'Happy?' Uncle Siegfried extended his cigar case and Wolz selected one of the familiar black cheroots. 'Who can be happy these days? Except in only the most personal and selfish way?'

'Personal, yes – but selfish? Aren't you entitled to grab what little of happiness you can when there's a war on?'

'I suppose – Lisl writes sometimes. Not about what she is doing. She does not sound particularly unhappy or happy. I get the impression she is under considerable strain.'

'We'll all come through, you'll see. The Wolzes always do –'

And then the mocking fact struck him shrewdly that

his own father, a Wolz, had not come through, smashed and trapped and sunk in his own U-boat right at the end of the last war. He chewed the cigar and it jutted up arrogantly from the corner of his mouth. 'Well, uncle — we are all coming through!'

# CHAPTER TWELVE

'Tower clear!'

The last of the water drained away through the scuppers from the free-flooding areas and Wolz slammed up the lid and clambered up on to the bridge. The watch followed in his wake with a heavy rush of bodies. The stars were still there, fat and sparkling and near, and the coast showed as a thin line low on the surface of the sea.

The warmth of the night struck him chill for a moment after the fug in the boat. Soon the night would be really cold. The desert was harsh; hot or cold, it imposed strains on a man.

They had the sea to themselves.

'Leutnant von Rohwer to the bridge!'

A moment later the Brandenburg appeared.

'Are we here?'

'I shall use the opportunity to instil a little more navigational instruction into the heads of my junior officers.' Wolz was perfectly serious. 'Leutnant Freyer and Fähnrich Thumen will take the star sights and work the plot. After that the position – I suppose I should say positions – will be checked by my First Watch Officer and myself. We can fix –' Wolz stopped himself.

He stared at the soldier.

'Would you care to take some sights and – ?'

'Yes.' Von Rohwer astonished him. 'I shall.'

When the sextant was brought up to the bridge the junior watch-keeping officer and the midshipman took their sights and made their calculations. The Brandenburg followed. Wolz looked at the positions marked out down on the chart. He grunted.

'If I was a betting man, and I am not; I wonder which one I should put my money on?'

The injured silence from his two junior officers made that evil black cigar jerk in the corner of his mouth.

'Number One! Find out where we are, will you.'

'Very good!'

When Ehrenberger finished, Wolz looked and that betraying cigar jerked. He looked up at von Rohwer.

'It seems you Brandenburgs are navigators, also.'

'We can turn our hands to many things. Out in the blue you have to navigate as you would guide a ship at sea.'

'Ah!'

The silence of the night breathed about them. The coast of Africa lay off their starboard bow. The starboard diesel just idled along, and they moved with the long sure swaying motion that told Wolz that Loeffler had U-55 running perfectly trimmed awash.

'We ought to reach the spot dead on time,' von Rohwer said. 'I am in your hands as to how you arrange that.'

'At this speed you ought to be picking up your landmarks inside half an hour. The Tommies certainly show a deal of light.'

That was true. Lights moved along the coast and the softened glare of lights from the west pulsed gently into the sky. But still the night around them remained silent but for the familiar noises of their own progress.

To the south the coast road trended inland a little and the Libyan Plateau south of that provided a kind of corridor between sea and scarp. Further east and south the Qattara Depression barred off easy access. All this land was under the control of the British. Wolz was most mindful of that as U-55 glided on through the shadowed sea under the stars.

His night's operations ough: to take him no nearer the beach than was prudent. He would be sending the airboat to the shore. There was no need to concern himself over the geographical peculiarities of the land. But, being Baldur Wolz, he liked to be on top of the situation and take cognisance of the lie of the land. That was second nature to him. Only the beach was of interest and the ruined tower which von Rohwer now sought through powerful night-glasses.

The Brandenburg's equipment had been brought up on to the bridge. Wolz gave the order for the airboat party to stand by. Von Rohwer struck Wolz as a man who knew what he was about.

The shore over there looked dark and dun and somehow ominous. And not just because it was swarming with enemy troops, either . . .

Through his powerful Zeiss Wolz scanned that dark shore. He picked up the jagged lump that must be the ruins just as von Rohwer said : 'There they are!'

'Clutches out,' ordered Wolz. 'Chief. We'll run on the electric motors. Keep your eye on the charge.'

'Very good!'

Loeffler would understand that U-55 slinking along on her electric motors would not make anything like the same amount of noise she would chunking along on her MAN diesels.

Von Rohwer nodded in satisfaction. He looked at his wristwatch.

'We have five minutes in hand. Excellent.'

If that was his idea of praise it suited Wolz.

'Silence in the boat,' Wolz made his voice neutral, matter-of-fact. He just didn't want raised voices floating across the stretch of water to listening hostile ears on the beach, and he did not want to put that order for silence into the same fraught bracket it was received when they were under depth charge attack and the English destroyers were listening out for them.

The five minutes ticked away.

From the beach, Wolz surmised, U-55 would look like a small matchbox afloat on the sea with a little frieze of round berries atop the outline. Trimmed down, that was all of the boat an observer would see. He was worried about von Rohwer's radio. If the man used it without due care and attention it could bring in half the RAF and the Royal Navy.

But von Rohwer knew what he was doing.

His blue-shaded lamp flashed twice, on and off, sending the dit-dit-da, dit-dit-da. U-U.

A few moments later a blue light flickered from the shadows da-da-da-dit, da-da-da-dit. B-B.

'Brandenburg,' said von Rohwer.

Wolz was perfectly aware of the tension. The men on the bridge breathed gently. They were just a little jumpy. No matter how many times you did this cloak and dagger stuff you always tensed up, always found nasty ideas of all the things that could go wrong running through your brain.

The sender of that blue-shaded signal need not be a German soldier. He could be a Tommy, with the Brandenburg patrol bound and gagged in the shadows, their secrets wormed from them, the blue light treacherously guiding a U-boat in for destruction . . .

He had to throw off these stupid fears.

This was just a job.

'Stop both. Bring us up, Chief. Stand by boat party.'

With a hiss of compressed air U-55 blew tanks and rose until her sleek casing broke through the water and glimmered iron and silver in the night.

Wolz continued to study the shore through the Zeiss.

If anyone was going to take a pot shot at them, now was the time. Or, better still, later when the airboat was on its way.

'Airboat party standing by, skipper.'

Wolz took the glasses from his eyes, blinked, and looked at Riepold.

'Very good. Remember, Ludwig, you'll be acting under Leutnant von Rohwer's orders when you're on the beach. In the boat – you are in command.'

'I understand, skipper.'

'Make it swift and clean and quiet.'

Von Rohwer turned.

'The High Command may regard North Africa as very much of a sideshow. Russia dominates their thoughts. Tobruk is a thorn in the flesh and, I believe I can tell you in all honesty, what my fellows are doing here will materially assist us in the very near future. I cannot tolerate any mistakes, Herr Leutnant Riepold. I am sure you understand me.'

Riepold opened his mouth. In the dimness Wolz saw his IIWO's face as a dark and, it seemed, empurpled patch.

'The Kriegsmarine will take care of you, Herr Leutnant,' he said, very smoothly.

'And the Panzergruppe Afrika will go through Egypt and reach the Caucasus and India long before the armies on the Russian Front.'

The passionate sincerity in von Rohwer's voice impressed Wolz. The plan was bold – it was audacious – but with a man like Rommel leading seasoned German panzer troops . . . It could be done!

It suddenly became vitally necessary for Wolz to fight down the irrational desire to go ashore himself. He wanted to take the airboat in and bring off these fellows of the Brandenburg. But, a captain could not leave his command just like that, when he felt like it, when a spot of bother might be expected. And Ludwig Riepold was a fine and dependable officer. Wolz would not forget the assessment he had made when he'd first met Riepold in that damned icy Norwegian fjord.

'Right. Prepare to launch airboat.' He stared at Riepold in the shadows. 'Remember – quick and silent!'

'Very good.'

Riepold went off with von Rohwer on to the casing. The airboat bobbed in the water and Hans Lindner was being cutting to the crew. Presently the boat rocked and then pushed off.

Wolz watched as the little craft paddled to the shore.

Thank God von Rohwer hadn't needed that suspect radio of his.

As the airboat neared the dun line of the shore Wolz had time to reflect that this von Rohwer was a bit of a fanatic. He had made no overt references to the party, as Jagow would have done in similar circumstances; he seemed to Wolz to be a fanatic for the army and the Third Reich. Well, much the same could be said for Wolz regarding the navy. The night breathed silently. The lookouts stuck to their posts, and there was nothing alarming to report.

The boat returned on its first trip and Wolz looked over the windbreak of his bridge as the soldiers came aboard. They did not clump about, and they moved with a lithe and alert precision that gave him hope they wouldn't clutter up his boat. They were shepherded below as the airboat set off again.

An Unteroffizier, bronzed, dark-chinned, festooned with weapons, showed his teeth in a smile as he went below.

'My thanks, Herr Kapitän. You provide the perfect end to a perfect party.'

Wolz did not reply and the soldier went down. Now what devilry had they been up to behind the Tommies' lines?

A small hum in the air, a distant buzzing, made Wolz lift his head. He looked inland. Yes – a distinct buzzing sound, as of engines. He automatically looked up. But, of course, it would be practically impossible to see aircraft in these conditions.

The airboat was making its second trip. No casualties had been reported so the full dozen soldiers would have to be embarked. The distant humming sound persisted and grew in strength. It was by no means a steady sound; rather, it rose and fell in a droning fashion.

In a strange and – if he admitted it – a somewhat worrying fashion that droning sound lulled him. He was tired. Well, of course, he was always tired on a patrol. That was a mere part of a U-boat man's life. He knew he would brace up to it when a moment of danger occurred, when the next emergency broke.

'What do you make of it, Kern?'

Ehrenberger tilted his head.

Even as he did so Wolz realised the sound was coming not from the land but from the shoreline away to the east.

'Engines, sir. Petrol – high speed – '

'Too fast for a lorry?'

'Decidedly.'

Wolz walked back to the stern of the bridge and looked down on the wintergarden.

'Stand by flak.'

'Very good.'

He went back to the front of the bridge. Again he lifted the Zeiss to his eyes. As he did so a flickering sheet of light, as of a door being opened on to a furnace and as quickly closed, raced across the dunes. He blinked. The sound of the volley reached him then, a flat series of crackles. Some of the light-streaks continued to flicker, and he knew they were Brens.

'A trap!' raged Ehrenberger.

'No.' Wolz stared at the confusing shadows, willing the airboat to reappear. 'If it had been a trap they'd have stopped the first parties. Hurry up, Ludwig!'

The gunfire from the beach was not being returned.

'Engage shore targets,' Wolz snapped and the 2-cm flak burst into action, slapping the little rounds in a spraying arc over the fire-points ashore. That would do little good; it would attract fire to U-55 and might just give the airboat a little edge . . .

'*Schnellboot!*' screamed the forward lookout. 'Dead ahead!'

Instantly, without need for thought, Wolz shouted at the flak crew.

'Cease fire!'

He leaped to the forward coaming and peered into the darkness. Two white wings, cleft by a sharp black prow, the flicker of metal beyond and then the shimmering creamy wash – an English motorboat, heading straight for them, and already beginning to shoot!

'Full astern both, full left rudder.'

Loeffler was quick. The motors thrilled their vibration through the boat as Wolz leaped back. He bellowed down at the 2-cm crew.

'Hit him as soon as he comes around! Don't miss.'

Even as Wolz spoke so the angry hornets of .303 fire sputtered and spattered over the boat. The bullets clanged and gonged from U-55's casing and conning tower. Where was that confounded airboat?

The party in the airboat would be the last. They might be the last, be too late. Wolz wasn't going to hang about if the English S-boat started tossing depth charges at him.

Ehrenberger popped up through the hatch.

'Skipper!'

The thrown MP38 was expertly caught.

Wolz looked at it for an instant as the night sky ripped apart under the onslaught of Lewis .303 rounds.

'What am I supposed to do with this Kern? Hit them over the head?'

Ehrenberger tossed his head back, swinging to loose

a clip in the general direction of the motor boat.

'It might discourage 'em, skipper – '

'True, true.'

Now U-55 was swinging under the urge of her twin rudders as Loeffler opened up the electric motors to the stops. The MGB swirled past and the instant the flak team caught that dark hurtling shape with the roaring white wings they opened up. Everything took only heartbeats. The English S-boat – the MGB – swerved in her dead flat run, her hard chine bouncing her over the water. She had two quad-Lewises hammering. She looked like an enraged bumble-bee.

Then shouts from overside dragged Wolz's attention.

The airboat was paddling up. Men in her were yelling. Bullets stitched the water about her as the Tommies continued to spray bullets indiscriminately from the beach. Now lights from a group of trucks suddenly opened up and began fanning weirdly across the dark water.

'You can douse those lights, Kern,' said Wolz.

'Delighted, skipper.'

Ehrenberger loosed off his machine pistol beachwards as the flak hammered away seawards where the MGB was turning in an enormous smother of foam.

A crewman on lookout duty abruptly screeched. He threw both hands in the air, clawing unavailingly at emptiness. He toppled forward and draped himself over the bridge. There was not much left of the back of his head.

Wolz bellowed, filled with so furious an anger he was shaking.

'Get those men aboard! Cut the airboat adrift! And pitch poor Schilling over the side. *Jump!*'

'Very good!'

The night was a bedlam of noise and flame. The soldiers of the Eighth Army continued to shoot from the shore as Ehrenberger sprayed MP38 rounds at the lights. The MGB swirled in again and cut loose with a long burst of Lewis-gun fire. And the flak 2-cm kept on chunking out shells.

Von Rohwer appeared. He held a bloody bandage to his face. Riepold pushed past, brisk and professional.

'All aboard, Skipper. Airboat cast off.'

'Chief!' yelled down Wolz. 'Open her up – give us everything you've got!' He was shaking. 'Full ahead!'

U-55 stopped reversing and her swing broadened. Now her bows pointed out to sea and towards the west. Useless to think of loosing an eel at the S-boat. It would be like trying to swat a fly with a flung half-brick.

The boat trembled as the MAN diesels opened up. Exhaust smoke coughed into the air, rank and raw. Bullets continued to clink and clang off the casing. Now the conning tower once more masked the 2-cm flak fire.

'Clear the deck!' rapped Wolz. 'Clear the bridge. Stand by diving stations.' He waited for just long enough. If anyone wasn't below when U-55 slid down then he'd be just too late. 'Flood! Dive!'

The drill went through like clockwork.

The English S-boat just could not be fitted with depth charges. Had she been so fitted they'd have been tumbled off already in one of the fierce passes. Then U-55 would already be sinking down, the air gushing from her fractured pressure hull.

He dropped down through the hatch and hauled it shut. The clàng came with the reassurance of a cathedral bell.

'Fourteen metres, Chief.'

At periscope depth U-55 slid along smoothly.

'Clear the soldiers out of the control room,' said Wolz, highly annoyed at all the sand-coloured uniforms. 'The PO's mess will take most of them and you'll have to stuff them in any odd corner. Up periscope.'

He took the usual quick three-sixty degree sweep.

The MGB, like an angry wasp, was circling, baffled. She hadn't slowed up that thirty knot assault-course speed once. Now she circled back, buzzing, going over their heads like an infuriating wasp dive-bombing a picnic party. Wolz ordered the scope down and felt, suddenly, a wash of weakness flow over him.

He should not have dived.

It had been an insane gamble to take. He couldn't be sure the MGB had no depth charges. Surely his own guns could have fought off mere .303 Lewises? But he'd seen the men hit in the airboat, and he'd seen Schilling with his head blown off, and he'd reacted as a U-boat man reacted.

He'd dived.

Maybe he was too tired, too drawn. Maybe he'd lost his sharp edge. Maybe he was over the hill. Maybe – he had no time to worry over what might be. He had a job to do and he just had to get on with it. These Brandenburgs had to be safely taken back.

And, the ugly question formed itself in his mind and refused to go away.

The doubt persisted.

*Had* his attack on the four coasters precipitated the situation on the beach?

Von Rohwer had no doubts.

Wolz was just saying: '. . . and have Sanitatsobermaat Otterndorf see to the Herr Leutnant – ' when von Rohwer stormed back into the control room. The scrap of bandage at his face dripped blood. He was icy with fury.

'Your conduct will be reported, Herr Kapitän! Make no mistake over that. The English were waiting for us on the beach – '

Wolz eyed him. He had been fully prepared to like von Rohwer, for a fighting man and a correct and courageous member of the Reich's armed forces. But this conduct ill-became a soldier.

'You have been wounded, Herr Leutnant. I am sure that is affecting your judgment – '

'I lost a good man, back there, and two wounded – '

'I, too, lost a man. A good man.'

'I warned you not to attack those coasters – '

'I do not think they affected the issue. It seems very obvious to me – '

'To you! Yes. But you were not on the beach.'

Wolz detested this. The whole scene degraded him in his own eyes. He slowly looked around the control room. Each man of the on-duty watch concentrated rigidly on his task. But they had ears. You couldn't cut those off. Enough damage had been done already. If he did as he wished and hauled von Rohwer off to his cabin to have this out in what privacy in the boat they could, these men in the control room would have heard half the story – the damaging half.

Wolz decided to have this thing out, here and now.

'Pass the word for Herr Leutnant Riepold,' he said, and the word was passed so promptly that Riepold appeared like a jack in the box.

'Skipper?'

'What was the situation on the beach when you landed?'

'All quiet. The Herr Leutnant made contact with his men and we loaded for the first trip.'

'And the second?'

'The same, skipper – '

Von Rohwer attempted to interrupt. Wolz turned an icy face on the soldier.

'Please allow me to continue, Herr Leutnant.'

'Very well.'

'Now, Herr Leutnant Riepold. When did the shooting start?'

'When we were loading for the third trip. One of the lookouts came in from the sand dunes – he'd been posted there as a lookout – and reported suspicious movements. He also said, skipper, that he believed the Tommies had been following them for the last couple of hours –'

'Impossible!' burst out von Rohwer.

'All the same,' said Wolz. 'This is an interesting development. Let's have this lookout in.'

'That will be impossible, Herr Kapitän!'

'Oh? Why is that?'

'He was the man who was killed.'

Wolz digested that. It tasted foul.

'I am sorry, Herr Leutnant von Rohwer. I regret the loss of a good man. But, perhaps his information was also known by others in the group?'

Von Rohwer nodded very stiffly.

'Perhaps. I will make enquiries.'

'Please do so. It is my considered judgement that the English would not have reacted in just this way to my attack on the four coasters. It is far more likely that your group was spotted as they descended to the beach. The Tommies readied themselves for the attack on that basis. Otherwise, they would have trapped the whole instead of the last party.'

Ehrenberger, who had remained silent, took it on himself to observe: 'And the English wouldn't know where to look for the boat that sunk the coasters. The manning of the entire coastline – well – that is not possible.'

'Thank you, Number One.'

Ehrenberger looked at Wolz, and away. But he'd put his oar in, and made his position plain in any subsequent enquiry.

'You had better let Otterndorf see to your wound –'

'A mere scratch –' protested von Rohwer.

'Nevertheless, please have it attended to – now.'

'Very good!'

At Wolz's crisp question, Willy Marwitz reported the hydrophone effect from the MGB to have disappeared. The sea held no hostile sounds. Wolz nodded with satisfaction. They'd lost men. The exchange had been made. He had lost Schilling for whatever devilry it was these Brandenburgs had got up to with the Tommies' supplies. Time to return.

'Take us up, Chief. Surface.'

The routine periscope check showed nothing. U-55 broke through into a quiet and starlit sea empty of menace.

# CHAPTER THIRTEEN

'Skipper!' said Loeffler, his red beard ruffled. 'That miserable air-intake valve. It's leaking again and it's looking to become nasty if we – '

'Will it hold out?'

Loeffler grunted. He was never one to exaggerate difficulties. This time Wolz waited for the answer to his question with a tinge of impatience. The anxiety he felt had been increased over the days of their run northwards, short though that had been, and he was beginning to feel that any more of these emergencies would be the last straw.

'It'll hold, Skipper. But what it's doing to my engines I don't like to think.'

Having all these soldiers as passengers did not help. They'd been stowed away in the feldwebels' mess, and in the spare bunk-spaces left by casualties. Even normally at full complement the men of a U-boat had to take turns sleeping, and some had to sleep on lockers between the bunks.

The ever-present condensation made everything wet to the touch. The food was just about to run out and they were being rationed for good drinking water. The hanging stalagmite jungle of sausages had shrunken to a mere miserable clump.

And, perhaps worst of all to Wolz as the commander, the heat of the Med was getting to the hands. They did not jump with the same old alacrity. They were sluggish. If U-55 were simply re-fuelled and re-supplied and sent off on another patrol . . .

But, then, Wolz could not bring himself to believe that would happen. They would have to have their extensive inventory of malfunctions put right. This last one, the leaking intake, was a wrong 'un, a real worry.

'Do what you can, Chief. It won't be long now.'

'I'll do what I can. As usual.'

As the LI went out of his cabin, Wolz reflected that the Chief was bearing up wonderfully well; but he, like them all, was showing unmistakable signs of cracking up.

That was no wonder.

The wonder was that men could continue to live and function under these frightful conditions.

It seemed to Baldur Wolz in those dark moments that all the familiar interior of his boat pressed in on him, a jagged mass of piping and levers and valves and dials, everything trying to collapse inwards and crush him to a red pulp.

Radio signals had conveyed his information, and orders to report back. The Brandenburg patrol had done well, he gathered, and officialdom wanted to make a bit of a fuss over his sinking of the light cruiser. Intelligence had now identified her as HMS *Melpomene*, of the *Dido* class, and a valuable anti-aircraft cruiser had been lost to the English Mediterranean Fleet.

The fact in the picture that irked Wolz was his remaining torpedo load. He had two up front and one at the stern, unloosed, just sitting there. They were why he came to sea, they demanded to be loosed into English merchantmen. But with things as they were the chance of that receded with every mile he neared base.

The tiredness ate into his bones. His joints felt inflamed. His eyes were granulated, red and angry-looking. Like them all, he stank. He kept his beard trimmed; but loose hairs presented a problem, and barbering had to be done on the surface according to his rule book. And the surface was beginning to become a strange place. It was a matter of popping up at night to recharge batteries, and of travelling submerged during the day.

The RAF flew unpleasantly active patrols.

Off and on he wondered what Italy was going to be like. If the German organisation hadn't as yet been able to equip a proper repair organisation he might be faced with a lengthy stay in Italy. The alternative, a return through the Strait and back to Lorient didn't bear thinking of.

He rubbed his eyes and winced. It felt as though sandpaper was lodged under the lids. He lay on his bunk, at least comforted by the thought that Ehrenberger had the watch and that dependable officer could be relied on. He felt the same about Riepold. Freyer was a trifle wild, at times, and would play his infuriating record; but he was shaping up. The whole crew of U-55 were tried and tested, tempered in battle. He would have to change some of them and would detest that all the way.

Mariza had spoken of that, of changing some of the crew.

He'd lost good men this trip, and Fahnrich Jagow was still in confinement, still as lunatic. Seeing men go mad in service in U-boats was no new thing; it would never be a thing to which you grew calloused.

Or, perhaps, if the war continued on and on and on — one day it would?

Well, there was one cheerful ray of light. Being stationed in the Med. would mean that BdU wouldn't be able to change his crew over so easily. It could and would be done, make no mistake, if it was thought necessary. Kernevel issued orders that were to be obeyed. But being so far from Kiel-Wik meant he stood a good chance of keeping his crew together. He found he very much wanted that. He needed familiar faces and well-known foibles around him, even Freyer's famous record . . .

He *was* tired . . .

He was not sleeping, he was not really awake. He drifted in a luminous rose-coloured cloud, swaying as he had swayed in the Bachstelze. He'd enjoyed flying the tethered kite trailed aft of U-42 and listening to Kapitänleutnant Gustav Ludecke's caustic comments over the phone. Ludecke had reported back to sea duty. Where he was now only God and BdU knew . . .

He caught a floating image of Mariza, naked and glowing, running fleetly through a forest glade, and of himself in hot pursuit. Hot was right. They'd had some glorious frolics.

'Baldur! There is a nasty branch sticking into my bottom!'

They'd rolled over and Wolz pulled the offending twig free. He tossed it aside, laughing, and caught up Mariza to him.

'And you're going away soon?'

'Yes.'

'Do you know where?'

'No idea.'

As though prompted by an inner compulsion, Mariza said: 'We are doing splendidly in Russia, aren't we?'

'Splendidly.' He traced a finger down between her breasts, feeling the silky-softness. 'But it is a big country.'

'Very big.'

'And so am I –' But she was up, laughing, shrieking at him over her shoulder, her hair flying, and they were off again, laughing and calling, racing between the tree were the sunshine flickered down like camouflage.

He did not think there'd be any home leave whils he was stationed in the Med. He was aware of U-55 abou him, solid and dependable and known – as dependabl as Loeffler could make her. She was really past it. Reall and truly, she ought to be pensioned off and be sen up to the Baltic to the training flotillas. Then he migh get a nice new shiny boat, a VIIC with a strengthened pressure hull so he could dive deep beneath the ghastly English wabos . . .

Just get the night over and he could bring U-55 safely in and order finished with engines and let her go to sleep. She'd be repaired, of course, and then he'd be off again. And, knowing himself, he knew he'd be chipper and bright-eyed and ready for the fray all over again. This dreadful tiredness would have been sloughed off. And, who knew what adventures awaited him in Italy? The Italians, unlike the French, were willing allies, weren't they?

He'd certainly take the opportunity to visit Florence and Rome and perhaps he might get down to Pompeii and Capri. That would be nice . . .

The alarm in the overhead squawked like a ruptured steam boiler.

'Kapitän to the bridge!'

Wolz was still half asleep as he fell off his bunk and charged from his cabin leaving the green curtain wildly fluttering. He crashed through the control room and up the ladder through the tower. Ehrenberger was staring off to starboard through his glasses and as Wolz clanged on to the bridge the IWO turned to him, snatching the glasses from his eyes.

'H.E. effect was reported, Skipper – diesels. And I'm sure here's a U-boat out there, running on the surface. I vish I could be certain I saw her – but . . .'

Wolz said nothing but took the glasses and stared along he indicated bearing.

The night breathed over the sea. The stars glowed. A uint of very early morning mist dampened out vision, laid a translucent cotton-wool gossamer over the sea. It looked hostly. Was that a shape, a long, low, dark shape, just ike their own?'

He took the glasses from his eyes but he did not rub hose inflamed pits of pain. He shut them, fighting the irritation, and then took another long careful look.

The sharp dark edge of *something* showed, creeping along with a wisp of vagueness defeating all further efforts to identify the shape.

Wolz made up his mind.

'Call the men to action stations, Kern. If it is a U-boat, and I think it is, it is not one of ours or an Italian.'

'I agree, Skipper.'

'Silence in the boat.'

Again Wolz looked. He was almost sure. He had to be absolutely sure before he committed himself. Low-voiced, he said: 'Clutches out. Chief – we may have ourselves something here. Group in and be ready to pick up on all four.'

'Very good,' came Loeffler's reassuring voice up the pipe.

'Steer oh-nine-oh.'

'Steer oh-nine-oh.'

As the diesel roar died and the electric motors grouped in so U-55's head began to turn to starboard.

'Prepare tubes three and four. Stand by.'

U-55 swung to starboard and her deadly bows began to line up. In the forward torpedo compartment the men were readying the last two forward eels. Wolz wanted to disgorge them. He dearly wanted to chalk this one up. But he had to be sure. Naval Group South would warn U-boat commanders of any possibility of a meeting in the approaches to base, and the Italians would likewise be informed.

As U-55 turned and like a lethal steel shark bared her fangs for the prey, Baldur Wolz felt absolutely confident that he would loose his eels at an English submarine.

'H.E. stopped, sir,' said Taffy Owens.

The diesel sounds he had picked up and whose bearing

and importance had brought Lieutenant-Commander Ray Bradbury, DSC, RN, on to the bridge in his usual avenging angel persona, nagged at Taffy's memory. His musical Welsh soul understood the nuances of sound. There had been a lilt, a beat, a special quality to that diesel ...

He listened as though his ears themselves extended out into the dark sea.

'Propeller noises, sir. Same bearing. But very faint – hardly hear 'em.'

Up on his bridge, Lieutenant-Commander Bradbury had the nasty feeling of déjà vu. All this had happened before. Only – it had not happened before. This was different, this was bloody well going to be different.

He looked along the bearing. The night was, as so often at this early time, deceptive. You thought you could see for miles, and all you were doing was gazing at a spot a few inches in front of your nose. Warm currents and cold, the hint of a breeze, atmospherics, they all played tricks.

'There he is,' he said. And the triumph in his voice was unmistakable. 'D'you see him, Webby?'

'Yes, sir – '

'Dive, dive, dive – and don't hit the bloody klaxon!'

They tumbled down. Bradbury had seen all he wanted to see from his bridge. He had seen – he had recognised, he had taken in that ugly shape which was supposed to look so much like the slim trim superb form of *Unscathed*. He knew what he intended to do and he just bloody well hoped he would get away with it.

These U-boat captains were bloody smart buggers.

'Periscope depth. Up periscope.'

The round eye on the outer world showed him nothing at first, and he was about to start cursing. The forward tubes were ready. He had two kippers left. He'd sunk a miserable little coaster and missed with a spread in atrocious circumstances and was determined to make the last two go in with a bang . . .

Ginger Everton kept his eyeballs glued to the big dial and his hands with the fine pelt of red hairs on their backs gripped the wheel with a delicacy of touch long training had made automatic. Sub-Lieutenant Pocock, pink-faced, was in the forward torpedo compartment and the sketchy training he'd endured that left him still a trifle shaky on the bridge had not skimped in this department. Bradbury had seen to that. Pocock knew how to handle the kippers, no sweat . . .

Giving himself a minimum period with periscope up, Bradbury took another look. And, this time, he spotted the ugly shape of the U-boat. It was swinging. No doubt of that, it was coming around. But Bradbury's immediate orders had taken *Unscathed* around, also, so that as the U-boat narrowed the angle, so *Unscathed* opened it again. Bradbury licked his lips.

The two submarines were pirouetting around each other like two dancers – or like a matador and a bull. The sword was poised.

The fruit machine did its duty and chunked out the figures; but Bradbury had the sublime conviction that he could aim this one with his eye and score a dead-centre gold.

Without doubt . . .

The tension in the boat reassured him. Everyone had a job and everyone did it. That ram-bow that was Bradbury's chin poked forward as he took the last sight. The deflection was right down, the range was perfect, and the fruit machine with its tiny cog-wheel and clockwork brain confirmed Bradbury's own aim.

'Fire one! Fire two!'

With an ominous hiss, two torpedoes sped for that ugly U-boat shape.

'Blowing sounds, skipper!' called Marwitz up the pipe.

'He's diving!' snapped Wolz. He stared at the slim distant shape and almost lost it. The angle was very fine. It would be a tricky shot – but if he did not loose now the Englishman would be gone and that would be the end of this stalk.

There was time. No doubt of it. His eels could reach in time – 'Loose! Loose!'

With an ominous hiss, two torpedoes sped for that ugly English submarine shape.

In the confusion of blowing tanks as his submarine dived there was a good chance the English hydrophone operator would not pick up those fatal torpedo propellers' sounds.

Time to dive . . .

Marwitz was yelling up the pipe.

'H.E. very loud! Bearing green sixty! Torpedoes running!'

'Dive!' yelled Wolz.

The bridge watch leaped for the hatch and tumbled down.

The electric motors were already running. The hatch slammed shut. U-55 started to go down. But without that extra kick from the diesels to start her on her downward plunge she was slower than the half minute she should take in an emergency dive.

One kipper hit U-55 aft, splitting open the watertight stern, flinging the screws and rudders and aft planes into shattered scraps of twisted metal.

The other kipper hissed into the pressure hull opposite the bulkhead dividing the electric motor room from the diesel engine room.

Black water roared in.

'Blow all tanks!' yelled Wolz.

The lighting flickered and the emergencies came on and Lindner had no need to go around screwing in fresh bulbs. Aft of the Petty Officers' quarters the U-boat was a mangled wreck.

But the batteries forrard were intact. Loeffler coupled in and blew tanks, and the bedlam of screams and the dark heavy rush of water was joined by the crazed hiss of compressed air. U-55 lurched and sagged into the sea.

'Abandon ship!' yelled Wolz. 'All out.'

The lights failed completely.

Utter darkness clamped down.

The sound of roaring water battered at their senses.

Forrard of the conning tower there were two escape hatches. Aft there was one.

The dragging feel of the boat thrust fear into every man of the crew. It gave their frenzied movements a desperate strength. Just who was first up the ladder through the tower Wolz did not know. But the men were pushing up the ladder, yelling and calling. A rubber watertight torch was thrust into his hand by Lindner.

'Thank you, Cox'n. We'll all get out.'

'Bound to, skipper. She hadn't really started to go down.'

'No.'

Wolz said: 'No.' But his brain screamed the thought: *But she is going down now!*

Some of the men ripped out the Drager Tauchretter escape apparatus. Lindner passed a set across to Wolz who put the life jacket over his head and pulled the notched strap up between his legs. The pipe and mouthpiece dangled free. All around him the noise of men struggling to escape filled the boat with hideous sounds.

The heavy beat of water continued to rush past. All aft of the feldwebels' mess was gone . . .

Poor old U-55 – due for pension – and now this . . .

He shoved the mouthpiece in between his teeth and bit down. The noseclip gripped his nose sharply, making him blink. With his right hand he reached down past the bag and twisted the tap of the oxygen bottle protruding through the side of the bag. He gave a quick spurt to check everything was working and blew a few times to clear his ears.

Loeffler came through and the torch picked out the ferocity of his red beard. Wolz took his mouthpiece out as the LI spoke.

'Helmuth,' he said, speaking savagely. Then, more correctly in the bedlam: 'Leutnant Freyer. He was pulped – gone to red pudding – '

'Up with you, Chief,' said Wolz.

The water thickened and the men had to fight their way up the ladders. U-55 was going down now, sinking, completely submerging. She was going down for the last time.

There'd be no more orders to blow tanks and rise. She was going down on her final descent.

No need to worry about the log he so painstakingly wrote up every day, if it fell out when he went up, that would be hard luck. No need to concern himself over the code books or the Enigma. They'd go down fathoms deep. He had done all a commander should do. His officers reported their sections clear. The hands called the commander Daddy among themselves; he liked that. They'd not call a commander Daddy if they didn't care for him.

The control room filled with water and emptied of men. The upper hatch had been thrown open in good time. Men were popping up out of the conning tower like bubbles from a sinking bottle.

The torch lit up the grimy bearded faces, the escape apparatus, the hair lifting in the water, the liquid gleam of fear in eyes turned to him. He sent them all up, one after the other.

Wolz was the last.

He cracked the oxy valve a little more and climbed the ladder.

U-55 began to roll as she plunged, going down stern first.

Just how far he would have to rise to reach the surface he did not know. The water surrounded him. Blackness smote him like a bludgeon. He had to remember to control his ascent. If he shot up he'd do himself damage with the nitrogen bubbles in his blood.

He did not fully remember doing all the things that as a commander he should have done; but he was the last. There was no one else left alive in U-55.

A tragedy about poor Freyer. But he would not be the only one. The personnel of the two engine rooms wouldn't have stood a chance.

As the water enwrapped him and both buoyed him up and sought to drag him down, he reflected that the captain of the English submarine had been very quick and very smart. But that was all over now. Wolz was not going down with his ship if he could help it. He had other boats to command, he knew that, and there were other girls waiting.

No – he had to get out and float to the surface. They'd be picked up by an Italian boat, that was certain. Wasn't it?

But he had lost his command.

The idea struck him a shrewd and cruel blow.

He clawed his way up through the hatch and in the pitch dark crabbed across between all the familiar artefacts of U-boat science on his bridge. Even in this blackness and under water he knew exactly where he was and what everything around him was and was designed to do. He held on to the attack periscope standard for a moment, setting the Drager, remembering the times he had looked through the lenses of this spargel to send his eels to destructive endings.

Well, this was not his own end.

Then he kicked off.

He said a mental goodbye to U-55. He had found her in a Norwegian fjord and he'd fought a successful war with her and now he said goodbye in the Mediterranean.

He went up through the blackness, controlling his rise, sucking in the oxygen and blowing, all as the drill-books said and as he had practised in the training base on the Baltic.

His thoughts tangled.

He had no real fear he wouldn't come through this lot alive. After he had been abandoned in the sea from his Bachstelze he had given himself up for dead, and now, in this kind of afterlife, anything was possible and he felt indestructible.

He'd have to go and see Lottie again. That new husband of hers was no good for her at all.

And Heidi, too . . .

As for Mariza, he wished he knew more of her, fine romp though she was.

And Trudi – Trudi von Hartstein. What was he to do with her?

The water lightened imperceptibly, pearling reluctantly, and turned soft and milky-green. The sun must be trying to poke through, then. It was almost daylight up there. The water was not really cold. Trudi . . . The next time he saw her he would take her in his arms and tell her – tell her – that she had to stop all this nonsense, whatever it was.

Lisl was barred. Very well – Trudi, yes, Trudi –

His head broke through the surface.

He blinked.

Other heads dotted the water and the sun's rays lay long and golden across the water.

He lay on his back, taking just a few more moments before he became a commander in the U-boat arm of the Kriegsmarine, even if he no longer had a command. He would have to collect the survivors, count heads, mourn the dead. They'd be picked up. He was supremely confident of that.

He looked across, away from the land, out to sea.

Two thin objects like pencils stuck out of the water. As he looked one disappeared and, a moment later, the other retracted and vanished beneath the surface.

Baldur Wolz breathed a long and furious gasp of anguished despair and fury.

The cheeky – !

That English submarine commander – poking around where he had just sunk a U-boat!

Just like the English, harebrained, stupid, brave, taking risks because they didn't have the foresight to plan for them. It had all been a great joke for that Englishman. Wolz knew that from long experience with his English friends. A party, that was how that English submarine commander would explain it when he got back to Malta. 'Just a spot of luck, sir. This jolly old U-boat popped up bang in front of me. Couldn't miss.' Oh, yes, Baldur Wolz knew about the English.

That was why he wished the Germans were not fighting them.

Cousin Siegfried and Cousin Manfred, in panzer and Messerschmitt – they were where a fellow ought to be in this war . . .

Baldur Wolz looked at the sea. But the English sub's periscope was not raised again.

He turned back to the survivors in the water – his men, his men of U-55. They'd take survivors' leave. They'd be retrained. They'd be given a new boat. He might even, surprisingly, be able to get away on leave and see Mariza again. And Trudi.

And, why then, in his new boat Baldur Wolz, Sea Wolf, might be off on another patrol . . . That was the way it would be.

There was no other way, not in this war . . .